Drained

E. H. Reinhard

AUTHOR'S NOTE

This book is a work of fiction by E. H. Reinhard. Names, characters, and incidents are products of the author's imagination or are used fictitiously. Any resemblance to actual events or persons, living or dead, is entirely coincidental. Locations used vary from real streets, locations, and public buildings to fictitious residences and businesses.

For more books by E.H. Reinhard, please visit:
http://ehreinhard.com/

CHAPTER ONE

Brett stood at his stove, tending a pasta dish in a pan. He had a number of small glass prep bowls filled with various spices and other things lined up on the counter. Soft jazz music was playing from the sound system in the living room. He wore a pricey gray dress shirt, unbuttoned at the top, with no tie. The fitted shirt held his muscular frame perfectly.

The doorbell chimed. Brett tapped the slotted spoon he'd been using to stir the pasta on the side of the pan and set it on the granite counter. He lowered the heat on the burner and walked toward the front door. He'd just buzzed his guest, Rebecca—or Becca, as she liked to be called—through the front gates a moment prior. He'd made every attempt and excuse to go and pick her up, but the woman was dead set on driving herself to his home, which was an inconvenience as he was running out of storage space.

Brett glanced through the door's peephole at her. She was wearing a loose-fitting black shirt that exposed her collarbones and a pair of short denim shorts. A purse hung from her shoulder, and large sunglasses wrapped her eyes. Her dyed blond hair was pulled back in a ponytail. He opened the door.

She smiled. "Hey. This is some place."

Brett smiled back and ran his hand through his perfectly manicured black-and-gray hair. "Thanks. Come on in. Perfect timing. The food is almost done."

Rebecca stepped into the house and looked around. "Wow. It's just as beautiful inside."

Brett smiled and closed the large front door at her back.

She took her eyes from observing the interior of the home and put them back on him. She stepped up to him, put her arms around his thick neck, and kissed him on the cheek.

Brett wrapped his arms around her thin frame.

"It's about time you invite me over," Becca said.

He chuckled. "Oh. What can I say? I like to take things slow."

Brett let go of the embrace and started for the kitchen.

She took the sunglasses from her chestnut colored eyes and rested them on her forehead. "The food smells wonderful. What are you making?"

He waved for her to follow him. "Linguine carbonara with cauliflower and pancetta."

She didn't respond but followed along.

"Grab a chair." He nodded toward the barstools around the kitchen island. "We have about two minutes, and we'll be ready."

"Do you need help with anything?" she asked.

He stirred the pasta and sauce. "Um, you could open that wine there." He jerked his chin at the bottle and the corkscrew on the kitchen counter.

"Sure. Glasses?" she asked.

He tapped the spoon on the edge of the pan and clicked off the burner. Brett pulled two wine glasses from the cupboard and set them next to her. He placed his hand on the small of her back and then ran it down her backside. "I'm glad you came," he said.

She looked at him and smiled. "I was actually starting to think you were married or something."

"Married?" he asked.

"I don't know. It just seemed like you are kind of hesitant, and…" She paused.

"And?" he asked.

"Only communicating through the website messenger system. That seems like something a married guy would do so he wouldn't get any messages to his phone." Becca twisted the corkscrew down into the cork and pulled it from the bottle. "So I'm going to come straight out and ask. Are you married?"

"No," he said. He held up his left hand and pointed to his ring finger, minus a ring.

"Girlfriend?"

"No, but there is someone I enjoy spending time with," Brett said.

She stared at him.

He smiled, showing his flawless dental veneers. "I was referring to you."

"Why, thank you. I like seeing you as well, John." She brushed her hand across his.

"Okay," he said. "Total honesty. I guess you could say I haven't had all that much luck with women in the past couple years, so I'm a bit cautious. As far as the phone thing, it already drives me up the wall with business. I try to limit who I give the number out to. But if you want my number, you can have it. I really don't have anything to hide. Program it into your phone."

Becca poured the wine and smiled. "Well, I would if my damn phone worked. It just quit on me a bit ago, right after I got your last message. It went black and wouldn't do anything. A couple minutes later, and it wouldn't even turn on."

"That's weird. Was it old?" Brett asked.

"No. I got it last year."

"Hmm, yeah, you didn't get it wet, did you?"

She shook her head.

"You didn't go and get a new one?" he asked.

"No. I didn't have time. I have insurance on it, so I imagine that they'll just give me a new one once I go to the store. I'm kind of hoping that it just starts working again without me having to deal with the hassle."

He nodded. Zero chance of that, he thought.

"Are these glasses going on the table there?" she asked.

"Yup. Let me just get this plated up quick." Brett pulled two plates from the cupboard and set them on the counter. He looked back over his shoulder. Becca had her back to him. Brett reached out and grabbed one of the small prep dishes filled with a powder and dumped it on one of the plates. He spooned a pile of noodles on top of the powder and spread it around. He grabbed a fork from the drawer and used it to fill his plate. He looked over his shoulder again. Becca was sitting at the table, looking back at him.

"Here we go," Brett said. He took the two plates and walked them to the table. He set hers in front of her and his plate at the seat across the table. He returned to the kitchen for some silverware and napkins. He handed Becca her utensils and took his seat.

"How in the world are you single?" she asked. "Great looking, you have all of this, you can cook…"

Brett shrugged. "I lead a pretty busy life with work. It doesn't allow me all that much time for a social life."

She nodded and looked down at her food. "It smells amazing," she said.

"Thanks. I've made this dish a handful of times before. It usually turns out pretty good, so we'll see."

"Do you cook a lot?"

"I guess you could say that." Brett took a sip of his wine. "I had a chef on staff to prepare meals for me a few years back. I watched what he was doing like a hawk. As far as my diet, I eat pretty well, which isn't really possible consuming things that are premade. This dish here I guess you could call a bit of a guilty pleasure."

She scooped up a forkful of the pasta and placed it in her mouth. She chewed and smiled. "It's delicious," she said.

He nodded. "Glad you like it."

She continued eating.

Brett picked at his food and watched her shovel forkful after forkful into her mouth. It took her the better part of twenty minutes to finish all but a few noodles on her plate. He gulped his wine down and went to refill his glass. "Did you want more wine?" he asked.

"Um, I guess," she said.

He walked the bottle back to the table and topped off her glass.

Brett retook his seat across from her as she lifted the

glass to her lips. Brett watched her hand waver on the way up, spilling some wine on the table. She didn't even notice she'd done it. Then she squinted hard and quickly shook her head.

"Something the matter?" he asked.

"Um, I don't know. I just got a little dizzy there." Her words slurred. She poked a piece of pasta with her fork and brought it to her mouth. She attempted to stab another, and the fork fell from her hand, clanked off her plate, and hit the floor. She tried to reach down for it and slipped from her chair to the tile.

Brett quickly went to her aid. "Let's get you back up," he said. He lifted her back onto the chair.

Becca pressed her hands flat on the table to keep herself steady.

"I think I know what might be the problem," Brett said.

She didn't respond, staring down at her plate.

"I said I think I know what might be the problem that you have going on right now." He waited for her to respond.

"Problem?" she asked. Her voice was low, and the single word took several seconds to come from her mouth.

"Yeah, it was probably the five milligrams of Rohypnol I put in your food."

"Ro... Rohypnol?" she asked.

"Yes. Rohypnol. I put it in your food to knock you out. You know how your phone stopped working? That's something I designed into the website app that gets downloaded onto your phone. It's actually part of the code in the messaging system. All I have to do is send you a specific message through the app, and it opens a virus which kills your phone. Cool, hey? That way, you couldn't be tracked here."

Becca didn't respond.

"You see. I'm going to kill you. I knew I was going to kill you from the second you responded. Every last thing you see is bait: the car, the house, the way I look, the way I dress and act. Everything has been put together to lure you in, to get you to this exact moment in time. Hell, I'd live in a trailer if I could. I honestly don't care about any of this stuff." Brett took a sip of his wine. "But apparently, you women do. They see someone single, in good shape, successful with money… Like moths to a flame."

Becca again didn't respond. She was facedown in her plate.

Brett shook his head, walked to her, and pushed her off the chair. Becca's limp body hit the floor, her head bouncing off the tile. He grabbed her by an arm and pulled her toward the stairs.

"Now for the fun part," he said. "At least for me." Brett reached out for the basement door.

CHAPTER TWO

My cell phone rang. I reached into my pocket and fished it out. The caller ID read Kane—my old partner, and technically my superior, at my last job at the Tampa PD. I clicked Talk.

"Hey, Captain. What's up?" I asked.

"Hank. How's it going?"

"I'm heading into the new office. Hoping this navigation in the car can actually get me there. It got me lost on Friday, so I'm taking a different route today."

"I see. So, are they putting you straight to work?" he asked.

"It sounds like it. I came in last week and met with the supervisor for the department. Seemed like he wanted to get me off and running right away."

"Special Agent Hank Rawlings," Kane said. "It still sounds weird to me."

"How do you think I feel?"

"So, did Karen buy you a bunch of new suits and dress you this morning? Get you all set for your first day?" He laughed on his end of the call.

"She might have picked me up a few things. Have to make a good first impression and all, or so she said."

"That sounds about right. So, how's the new house?"

"Boxes and mayhem. Porkchop bouncing around, doing his best to constantly be underfoot. Karen being emotional. So pretty much the same as in Tampa, plus boxes."

"Speaking of Karen, has she started yet?" Kane asked.

"Yeah, beginning of last week. She seems to act like she likes it so far. Same job, just a bigger division. One second, Kane. The car's nav is giving me some directions here."

"No problem," he said.

My navigation instructed me to take the exit in one mile and told me the name of the exit. I put on my directional and got to the right lane. As soon as I did, my navigation stated that it was rerouting. The woman's voice, along with an arrow on the screen, told me that I'd arrived at my destination. I poked my finger at the navigation screen in the car's dash, and it went black aside from the time in the upper-right corner. Then the middle of the screen said Calculating.

"Calculating? What the hell does that mean?" I asked.

"What?" Kane asked.

"Nothing. My navigation is doing something I've never seen before and also apparently doing whatever it can to get me lost."

The car behind me honked. I glanced into my rearview mirror and saw the grille of a sedan inches from my rear bumper. I looked down at my speedometer—I'd slowed to forty-five miles an hour. I exited the freeway on the ramp I'd been originally directed toward and pulled to the shoulder of the off-ramp. The guy in the sedan gave me the middle finger as he passed.

"Jerk," I said.

"Freeway trouble?" Kane asked.

"Huh?"

"Sounded like someone was getting some use out of their horn."

"Oh, yeah, whatever. Just someone who doesn't know how to drive," I said.

"You or the guy honking at you?"

I dismissed the jab. Kane had never been a fan of my motoring skills and always insisted on taking the driving duties when we were out on a case. "Yeah, yeah. So what's up?" I asked.

"Nothing. Pushing a desk. Staring at spreadsheets," he said.

"Sounds exciting. Did they find you a lieutenant yet?"

"Soon," he said. "Jones and Donner both took the test. Plus a couple of guys from different districts. I should know something within a week or so."

I caught the time on my watch. "Hey, let me give you a buzz tonight or tomorrow to shoot the shit. I'm going to need to run here to try to get to work on time."

"Yeah, no problem. Whenever you get a minute," Kane said.

"Tell the gang I said hi," I said.

"Will do."

I clicked off and slid my phone back into my pocket. Then I poked my finger at the car's navigation screen. The Calculating message disappeared, and the screen lit back up with the map.

"Okay, let's try this again." I punched in the address

for the Manassas, Virginia federal building. The route came up, and the robotic woman's voice told me it was just two and a half miles away. I shifted the car back into drive and continued on. My new workplace came into view on my right just a couple minutes later. The federal complex consisted of two matching white five-story rectangular buildings separated by a six-story curved central building with a lannon-stone facade. I pulled into the complex and stopped at the guard building. One man, armed with a rifle, stood just outside the small building, and another slid open the building's window.

"Identification," the man said from inside the guard shack.

I pulled my credentials from my suit jacket's inner pocket and handed them to him.

He scanned the bar code on the ID and handed it back. "New, huh?" he asked.

"Yes, sir," I said.

"Well, have a good day, Agent," he said.

I gave him a nod, watched the guard shack's security barrier rise, and proceeded to the parking lot. I found a spot, bounced off the parking curb, and killed the motor. Small shrubs and light posts lined the concrete walkway as I headed up the long curved sidewalk to the central building's main entrance. I pulled open the front door and entered. My feet clacked against the white tile floor. The walls and ceiling were also white, the only color in the room coming from potted trees, more of the same lannon-stone facade carried over from the front of the building, and a blue section of wall with the FBI logo in the center. I made my way to the bank of elevators in the right corner, rode up to floor two, and stepped off. Agents in suits hustled back and forth around the cubicle-filled office. I was standing in the main room of the serial crimes unit. It looked more like a computer tech company or maybe a stock call center. It definitely didn't resemble law enforcement—maybe it was all the suits instead of patrol uniforms. I headed toward my department, nodding hellos to those I passed. The homicide unit was across the office and through a door near the back. I made my way there, twisted the knob, and walked in. I closed the door behind me.

I looked left to right across the department. Immediately to my left was a large office with the blinds drawn. It belonged to Supervisory Special Agent Art Ball, my superior, who I'd met with the prior Friday. The office was dark. On the right wall were two rooms—the one closer to me was the tech center. That room was filled with computer monitors and desks. I saw no one inside. The second room to the right, where I'd been told the morning meetings would be conducted if necessary, was much larger. I walked toward it and glanced inside. The lights were on, with no one there. Standing bulletin boards filled with photos took up most of the back wall. A large rectangular table ran straight up the center. I rounded the corner to the right. Four agents' desks, including mine, were lined against the left and right walls of the room. Another office with the door closed and the lights off took up the rear wall.

A single female was sitting and staring at a computer at the far desk on my right. She was gnawing on the end of a pen, but she set the pen down and spun in her chair to face me as I walked toward the empty desk I'd been assigned directly behind her. I showed her a smile. I'd seen the woman as I left the other day but hadn't been introduced.

"I'm guessing you're our newest addition?" she asked. "It's Hank, right?" She stood from her desk and walked to me with her hand outstretched. She was strikingly attractive and looked to be in her late twenties or, at most, thirty. She had an athletic build—at least, it looked athletic from what I could tell. Her hair was a few inches past shoulder length and dark brown. The woman wore a gray pair of slacks and a matching gray blazer over a white top.

I'd been known to hold a stare a bit too long and felt that may have been one of those occasions. I quickly reached out and shook her hand. "Yup. Hank Rawlings. You are?"

"Beth Harper."

"Nice to meet you, Agent Harper."

"Just Beth. All of us in here keep it pretty casual."

"That works for me," I said.

"You were from Florida, right?" she asked.

"Tampa," I said.

"And…" She paused in thought. "PD homicide sergeant?"

I nodded. "Seems like you've been informed about me."

"It's always good to know who you'll be working with," she said. "So did you get the position and then move up from Tampa, or…?"

"Well," I said. "My wife works with the DEA. They transferred her to Arlington. As soon as we found out about the transfer, I started looking up here. Figured I'd try the Bureau before looking into local law enforcement."

"Ah," she said. "Well, you must be good. We don't see

a lot of people come straight into the more desirable units from law enforcement."

"More desirable units?" I asked.

"Yeah, the serial crimes unit and subunits that fall under it are kind of what everyone wants. It took me like three years to get into this unit. Most of the other agents longer. What are your qualifications?" she asked.

I was silent... in thought. I wondered if I'd be resented for being underqualified in the eyes of my peers. The truth was, I had been granted an interview; had received a conditional offer of employment; had gone through all the processing, including polygraphs and medical; and had been offered the spot. I'd been checked and rechecked. The process took over two months. Apparently, those in charge thought I was qualified enough. Her asking about my qualifications was a little off-putting. I pushed the thoughts away and figured I'd do my best to show her I had enough background for the position.

"Well, I've been in homicide for a bit over ten years, and as far as college—"

She swatted my shoulder, interrupting me.

"I'm just screwing with you. Relax a bit, Hank. Ball likes his team to be bits and pieces from everywhere. If you've made it through everything, I'm sure you'll be a great addition. I do have a serious question for you, though."

"Shoot," I said.

"When you got up this morning and got ready to come in, did you actively try to see how close to the stereotypical FBI-agent look you could get?"

I was quickly getting a better bead on Beth's personality though I wouldn't immediately tell her about

Karen picking out my clothes for the day. I puffed up my chest and tightened my tie. "How am I doing?"

She smiled. "You're damn well nailing it: a few inches over six foot, a few pounds under two hundred, early forties, dark hair with a touch of gray, clean shaved. The black suit and tie with a white dress shirt completes the look. You are one hundred percent the standard FBI agent to the T."

"See, I'm already doing my job," I said.

She laughed and walked past me. "Come on."

"Where are we headed?"

"Do you drink coffee?"

"Of course," I said.

"Let's go grab one. I'll show you a couple things around this place before the rest of the team gets here."

"Sure," I said.

She headed for the door. I pulled up my jacket sleeve and looked at the time on my watch—a few minutes past eight. "What time does everyone start filing in?" I asked.

She reached out for the doorknob. "About nine or so. No punch clocks in our division. Ball likes us in by nine thirty at the latest and likes us to stay until"—she deepened her voice and did a manly impression of our supervisor—"you can look yourself in the mirror and say, 'I've done my job for the day.'" She chuckled. "Sorry, I don't know how many times I've heard him say that. I usually leave around five. The other agents that show a little later stay a little later."

"Sounds fine," I said.

She opened the door and waved over her shoulder for me to follow. "That's just if we're cold. If we're on something hot, well, that's a different story."

15

"I'm assuming cold and hot are in regards to cases?"

"Well, we call them investigations, but yeah, same thing."

She turned left down a white hallway in the center of the large room filled with cubicles. I followed.

She continued speaking over her shoulder. "*Cold* is something where a new body hasn't been found in over a year or where we suspect there is an active serial killer that may not be actively killing at the moment. *Hot* being we have active killings and need to be on location."

"I see," I said.

She made a right through a doorway. Four long rectangular tables filled the room. Behind the tables were various vending machines and a long counter. The counter was filled with boxes of donuts and bagels. A few dishes of fruit and a row of commercial-looking coffee machines spanned the wall. She headed toward the coffee.

"We go hot about once every other month," she said.

"That often, huh?" I asked.

"Yup. Did you ever hear the thing that there are like fifty serial killers considered active inside of the United States at any given time?"

"Yeah, that sounds vaguely familiar," I said.

She grabbed a cardboard coffee cup from the rack and nodded for me to do the same. I did and stuck it into the machine then pulled the lever down to fill the cup from the spout.

"Okay, well, that number is complete bullshit," she said. "Maybe multiply that by five or ten. The truth is we don't know for certain and never will. Our job is to do our damnedest to remove as many as we can from the population. Have you worked a serial-killer case before?"

"Multiple in the last year," I said.

"Just Tampa?" she asked.

"Yeah."

"How long was each case?"

"A week or two, with all suspects in custody or deceased." I pulled my full cup of coffee from the machine and blew across the top. When I took in a mouthful, the flavor was surprisingly good.

"Spree killers," she said. "Well, technically, they are still serial killers, but they are a little different breed. Those get to us every now and again, but usually spree killers end up getting caught by local police or local branches of the bureau. When you dump a bunch of bodies in a short period of time in a single area, the odds of getting caught are pretty much a certainty. The cases we get generally have to pass through the local level. Basically, the killers have been active for longer without being found." She pointed at the donuts and bagels. "Grab something."

Beth took a seat at the table nearest us.

I patted a pocket in my suit jacket. "The wife sent me out with a couple of power bars." I pulled one out, unwrapped it, and took a seat across from her. "So, what is the day-to-day like here?" I asked.

Beth sipped her coffee. "I guess you could say we operate like a cold-case division would unless we're on something."

I nodded. "How many in our unit?"

"Seven now... and Ball. Jim Robinson handles all of our records, paperwork, travel, warrants, and things of that nature—he's mostly tied to his desk. Lewis and Marcus are our tech twins. Bill and Scott are field agents, along with you and me. Bill is off on vacation, though. I don't think he comes back until sometime next week."

I pulled out my notepad to jot down the names of my coworkers. I figured at least knowing their names would be a decent start at a first-day-of-work impression.

"How many units like us are out there?" I asked.

"You mean serial crime units with the specific homicide tag?" she asked.

"Yeah," I said.

"Serial crime units are everywhere," Beth said. "As far as devoted to strictly homicide, just us and another unit on the west coast."

CHAPTER THREE

We headed back into our unit office. The lights in Ball's office were still out, but I caught movement inside the tech room. Beth headed for the door, turned the knob, and walked inside. I followed. The room consisted of two cherry-colored desks that took up the better part of both walls on the left and right. With a quick glance, I counted eight monitors per desk. A thin rectangular table with eight chairs ran down the center. The back wall of the room was four larger monitors at different angles, computer towers, and miscellaneous office equipment.

"Lewis, Marcus," Beth said, "come meet our newest edition."

The two rolled themselves away from their desks in their office chairs, stood, and walked over. I noticed that on their desks were what looked like matching iced coffees. As the pair approached, I saw why she called them the tech twins. Both looked to be in their midtwenties, both had short blond hair and blue eyes, and both wore dark polo shirts and khaki slacks. They looked as though they should be trying to sell me a television in an electronics store. The one on the right held out his hand toward me.

"Marcus Phillips."

I shook his hand. "Hank Rawlings."

The one on the left held out his hand toward me next.

I took it. "Hank Rawlings," I said again.

"Lewis Phillips."

I looked at him and then the other. Hair matched, eye color matched, apparel matched, and last name matched.

"We're not related," Lewis said. "Just a coincidence that we have the same last name."

"We actually think they may have been separated at birth," Beth said. "We're going to look into it one of these days."

"Yeah, yeah, ha ha. We look nothing alike," Marcus said.

"Keep telling yourselves that," Beth said. "So what are you two on today?"

"Hunting down cell-phone coordinates for someone Scott was interested in. We'll see where that goes," Lewis said.

Beth turned her attention to Marcus.

"Still working on those credit-card purchases and associated video that you requested. I should have everything by the end of the day," Marcus said.

"Thanks," Beth said. "We'll leave you guys to it."

We walked from the tech office back toward our desks. "Seems like they keep busy," I said.

"They're surprisingly good when they're not looking at dumb videos or reading tech articles online."

"Sounds like my old tech department," I said.

"I think it comes with the profession."

She pointed at a man at the desk one over from mine as she took a seat at hers. "This is Scott. Scott, this is our newest, Hank."

He stood from his desk. The man was roughly my size in height and weight though I imagined he had a few years on me, from the crows' feet at the corners of his eyes. He wore a gray suit with a white undershirt and a maroon tie. His hair was dark and finger length on the top while the sides were shorter and graying. I stepped toward him and shook his hand.

"Scott Mathews," he said.

"Hank Rawlings."

"You were in law enforcement, correct?" His voice carried a northeastern New England accent.

"Tampa homicide sergeant," I said.

"I used to work violent crimes in Boston until about two thousand five, when I came here. I was a detective." He smiled. "I'm sure we'll have some stories."

"Without a doubt," I said.

"Well, I was just heading off to grab a coffee. We'll chat more later."

I nodded. He passed me and walked out. I sat at my desk and took in my new surroundings. A computer monitor, mouse, and keyboard were directly before me though I had nothing to use the computer for. I continued checking out my work area, which was far nicer than my metal desk in the center of the Tampa PD bullpen. My workstation was cherry colored and the better part of five feet long. Slots for files and folders were attached to the wall—all empty. I slid out the drawer beneath the computer keyboard—also empty. I'd been given nothing to work on and had no clue what I should have been doing. I wasn't a fan of the feeling. I turned in my chair. "Beth, do you need a hand with something?" I asked.

"Um, I think I'm good. Ball will give you a few things to start with when he gets in." She responded without turning around.

I went back to staring at a blank work area. I wiggled the computer's mouse. A blue screen with an FBI logo popped up. A rectangular box below the logo on the screen asked for a login and password—I had neither. I turned in my chair and looked toward Ball's office. From my spot, I could just see the door and blinds of his office from around the corner. He still wasn't in.

Someone rounded the corner as soon as I was about to go back to staring at my blank desk. His eyes locked on me. The man looked to be in his later sixties. He was African American with short white hair and a short white beard. He stood an inch or two over six foot. I put his weight around one eighty. The man wore a tan sports coat over a patterned shirt—no tie. Under his right arm was a folder. He walked directly toward me.

"Are you Agent Hank Rawlings?" he asked.

"I am," I said.

"Good. I found you. We're going to need to do a little follow-up here on your psych evaluation. It looks like we have an abnormality."

"Um." I paused. "Abnormality? What does that mean?"

"A few conflicting things on our test results that we'll have to get ironed out before we can have you active."

"All right. Well, what do we have to do to get this straightened out?" I asked.

"We'd like to administer another polygraph and have

our panel compare the results against your previous one." The man stood next to my chair, staring down at me as I was seated. His face showed no emotion.

I glanced over at Beth to see her spinning her chair back toward her computer. She appeared to want no part in the conversation the man and I were having.

"Um, okay, I guess," I said.

"It should take about six hours," he said.

"Yeah, sure, if we need to."

Beth snorted. I glanced over at her and then back up at the man.

The corner of his mouth turned up into a smile. "Sorry," he said. The man snickered. "What fun is life if you can't mess with the new guy? Jim Robinson." He reached out for a handshake.

I shook my head, smirked, and gave him a handshake. "Good to meet you," I said.

"I take care of the records around here," he said. "Well, that and pretty much everything else. Travel arrangements, hotel bookings, warrants, you name it."

"Good to know," I said.

He turned his attention to Beth. "Beth, Ball has something for you. You were on the bodies found drained of blood from years back, right?"

Beth spun on her chair and faced us. "Yeah. Why? Something new?"

"It looks like he's active again."

"What? No one told me anything about that," she said. "There hasn't been a new homicide that we could attribute to him for what, like eight years?"

"Ball just got the word early this morning, I guess. I passed him on the way in, and we spoke a bit. I'm sure he'll be briefing you on it shortly." He looked back at me. "Good to meet you again, Hank—and welcome."

"Thanks," I said.

He walked toward his office.

Beth flashed a concerned face and turned back toward her computer.

Scott returned from getting his coffee and took a seat beside me at his desk. The only agent I had yet to meet from the team was Bill, yet it had sounded as though that wouldn't happen for a good week or so. I glanced down at my watch, and the time was inching up on nine thirty. I looked back up to see a man in his early fifties and of average build staring back at me. His suit was gray, his undershirt light blue, and his tie a darker shade of blue. An American-flag pin was affixed to his lapel of his suit jacket. He had styled gray hair and was clean shaven. He held a couple of folders under his right arm.

"Beth, Hank, meeting room," Ball said. He turned and disappeared.

Beth scooted herself back from her desk, and I did the same. I followed her around the corner and into the conference room. Ball stood at the doorway and saw us in. "Grab a seat," he said.

We funneled in and sat.

"We have more bodies drained of blood?" Beth asked. "Same guy?"

"It looks like it." Agent Ball set down the folders he was carrying on the table and looked at me. "I'm assuming you've met Beth here?"

"I have," I said.

"Good. You and I will get together as soon as we're done here and go over some other things."

I nodded.

"Okay, let's get down to business." Ball handed both of us a file.

I took the folder in my hands and flipped it open. The cover sheet read SK 138. I assumed SK stood for "serial killer." I flipped another page in to see photos of a deceased woman lying in a Dumpster, and the next page was an autopsy report and more photos. I kept flipping pages. A copy of the woman's driver's-license photo and personal information came next. She appeared to be from a Chicago suburb. The following pages looked to be sheets from interviews with friends and family. I flipped another page—photos of a different woman in a Dumpster and then another—three total. The last two victims were three weeks apart and also from the Chicago area. The last victim had been found just two days prior.

Beth spoke up. "These dates…" She thumbed through the pages. "Looks like the first one was a month ago. Why didn't I hear about this?"

"The local PD never reported it to the bureau. The second two were dumped in the same precinct. They called the bureau after the second victim. The bureau found out about the first in the other precinct, put it together, connected the dots, and notified us."

I flipped to the pages of the autopsy reports and ran my finger down the page to the cause of death. I looked up at Ball, standing on the far side of the table. "Drugged and drained of blood?" I asked.

He nodded.

"Yeah. The draining of the blood was this guy's MO when he was active years ago," Beth said. She flipped to another page in her file.

"Appears it still is," Ball said. "They found Rohypnol in each woman, which is new. A lot of Rohypnol. It looks like about four or five times what it would take to incapacitate someone. The body dumps are all similar—basically, someplace off the beaten path where there's a Dumpster. The draining of blood is done by needles—it's consistent with victims past."

"Nothing to connect the victims?" I asked.

"There never was on the past victims," Beth said.

"The new ones?" I asked.

"The local branch is just getting rolling with the most recent ones, but so far, no," Ball said.

"How many victims were there before?" I asked.

"Thirteen total now," Ball said.

"Do we have files from the previous victims?" I asked.

"We do, and I'll give them to you to look over. Those files have been gone over who-knows-how-many times, though," Ball said.

"Okay. Were there ever any suspects with the previous killings?" I asked.

"Not a single one, as far as I recall," Beth said.

"Keep in mind we didn't have the technology then that we do now for hunting people down. It's a lot harder to hide now than it was even eight years ago," Ball said.

"Any idea how he was selecting his victims?" I asked.

Ball looked at Beth to field the question.

"I think I remember there being theories in the original files, but that's it. Nothing was ever proven," Beth said.

I nodded and looked at Ball. "You said the local branch of the bureau was working on this... How far are they into the investigation?"

"The Chicago branch is actively investigating it but

only a couple of days in. They requested us as it's an open investigation through our department. I told them we'd be at their office tomorrow." Ball looked at me. "Trial by fire?" he asked.

"I'm up for it," I said.

"Okay. Beth, this guy is one of yours, so…"

"Absolutely. I'm ready to go," Beth said.

Ball looked at me. "You guys will fly out in the morning. Jim will arrange everything for you. That's it. Rawlings, you come with me so I can get you set up on a few things. After that, Beth can get you up to speed on everything we have regarding the previous homicides attributed to this guy."

"Sure," I said.

We disbanded and left the office.

CHAPTER FOUR

Brett sat at the breakfast bar in his kitchen, wearing a pair of boxer shorts and a white undershirt. He was fresh from the shower after his daily morning workout. He was just about through with his breakfast—a grapefruit, two eggs, and a chicken breast. He washed down each bite with a gulp of a protein shake. Brett glanced at the clock on the oven—a bit after nine. He'd need to get moving if he wanted to be in the office on time for his first meeting. He lifted the last forkful of chicken to his mouth, chewed, and washed it down. Then he rinsed his plate, set it in the dishwasher, and from the counter, grabbed a piece of paper he'd printed. He made for the basement stairs.

Brett walked downstairs. The lower level of his home was completely furnished, his own personal man cave. The main room held a pair of pool tables, a foosball table, and a pair of dartboards against the left wall. A large bar shaped in an L took up the far right corner. He walked past the large theater seats facing a huge television in the center of the wall next to the bar. A single door stood in the middle of the large room's back wall. The door led to a short hallway. His home gym was to the right, a sauna to the left. Brett continued past them to another door leading to an area of unfinished basement reserved for storage. In the far left corner of the unfinished side of the basement was a washbasin, some miscellaneous shelving, and his washer and dryer. To the right side was a flight of stairs leading up to the garage. He walked over toward the washbasin and the stainless-steel embalmer's table standing before it.

Brett reached for a roll of tape on a shelf. He tore off a two-inch piece and taped the paper he'd printed next to others like it on the wall. Brett put on some blue rubber kitchen gloves that were sitting on the edge of the washbasin.

He looked down and to the left. Becca lay in her undergarments on the embalming table. Needles with tubes attached came from both sides of her neck, both arms, and both thighs. The clear plastic tubes held a bit of blood, but most of it had already drained into the basin under Brett's watchful eye the night prior. Brett liked to keep the needles in overnight though the women generally drained within minutes of having them inserted. Becca was dead and had been that way for at least twelve hours.

Brett pulled the needles from her neck first, then arms, then legs. He lay them inside the washbasin, where he would thoroughly clean them at another time. He turned and grabbed a bottle of bleach and a sponge from another shelf on the wall. He doused the woman's body and began scrubbing, head to toe. When she was cleaned to his satisfaction, he rinsed her down to wash the bleach away. He took his old Polaroid camera from the shelf, snapped a photo, and pulled it from the camera. Brett shook it in his hand and set the camera back on the shelf. When the photo finished developing, Brett paper clipped it to the page he'd just taped to the wall.

He turned and walked back upstairs to get ready for work, planning to dispose of her when he found a suitable time.

CHAPTER FIVE

I walked in the front door of our red-brick Arlington townhouse. Karen and I had been a little sticker shocked by the cost of property in the area, so we were opting to rent prior to purchasing. I wasn't the biggest fan of someone living attached to us, but I told myself it was temporary.

"Porkchop!" I called.

I heard thumping puppy feet and the scratching of bulldog nails on the wood floors of the second story. I heard his usual controlled fall down the steps. He turned the corner where the stairwell met the hallway before me. He slid, brindled butt first, into the wall as he turned the corner. His paws swiped off of the hardwood as he tried to gain traction running toward me down the hall. I knelt for my welcome-home greeting. He ran full out toward me, locked up the brakes a few feet short, and slid to a perfect stop in front of me. He licked and slobbered and barked as he received his petting. Then I stood and headed into the townhouse. Porkchop walked directly at my knee. "Come on. Outside," I said.

I opened the sliding glass door at the back of the house and let him out into the fenced-in backyard, leaving the door cracked open. I knew he would return when he finished doing his business. I tossed my car keys and phone onto the kitchen table, and I caught the time, a bit after six thirty. Karen would be home any minute.

Porkchop reappeared from outside and came to my feet.

I reached down and gave him a scratch behind his ears. He stared back.

"Were you a good boy today?" I asked. "Let's go find out before your mother gets home."

I did a quick lap around the lower level while Porkchop followed. I didn't see any puddles on the wood or anything chewed on. None of the boxes stacked in the corners looked disturbed.

"Halfway there, dog," I said.

I headed upstairs to give the second story a once-over. Porkchop raced me up the steps and won. I looked over the master bedroom, office, and spare bedroom—again, dog-trouble free.

I stopped in the hall after checking the main upstairs bathroom and looked down at Porkchop. "Well, holy shit. You made it through the day without doing anything naughty. I'm impressed."

He looked at me and cocked his head to one side.

"Okay, come on, let's go get you some dinner with a few treats sprinkled on top."

He didn't respond.

"It's dinner time."

Porkchop spun in a circle around my legs. He knew the words "dinner time." He liked dinner time.

"Do you want some treats?" I asked.

He about went back-over-front, tearing down the stairwell toward the kitchen.

I headed for the steps, went back downstairs, and fed the dog. The food was vanishing before my eyes in a few seconds.

"Chew," I said.

He didn't.

The sound of the front door opening and closing caught my ear and the dog's. I left the kitchen and turned into the hall. Porkchop was already at my wife's feet.

Karen knelt and scratched him behind the ears. "Hey, buddy," she said. Karen looked up at me. "How did he do today?"

"I didn't find anything anywhere," I said.

"Good job, Little Chop." Karen continued petting the dog.

"How was the drive today?" I asked. "I heard the traffic guy on the radio on my way home. It sounded bad."

Karen stood. She wore a gray blazer over a lighter-gray shirt and matching slacks. A multicolored necklace hung from her neck. She kicked off her shoes at the door. "The traffic was brutal," she said. "It took me damn near an hour to get ten miles." Karen freed her black hair from a bun. It fell a few inches past her shoulders.

I walked over and gave her a hug and a kiss. She was holding a brown bag of groceries in her arm, so I took it from her. "What did you get?" I asked.

"Organic chicken and spinach plus a few other things. Basically, everything to make chicken Florentine."

"I thought we were done with the organic kick?" I asked.

"Nope. I found a nice little market."

I nodded but said nothing.

"I figured after dinner we could go out and see the town a bit. Maybe do a little dancing," Karen said. It sounded more like *this is what we are doing* as opposed to *I would like your input on the topic.*

Karen enjoyed control, which after almost twenty years of marriage, I'd gotten accustomed to. She seemed to honestly like being in charge of the little things, from food to vehicles to entertainment. The big things in life we always discussed. The truth was while I'd often get crap about my wife wearing the pants, not having to worry about the little things made my life a lot less stressful, and as much as I could take or leave dancing the night away, it made her happy, which made me happy. Karen could still get a little carried away at times, but as far as our marriage went, I don't think we could be a better pairing.

"Um, about going out," I said, "shouldn't we probably deal with the boxes and start getting things organized instead?"

"It can wait," Karen said.

I shrugged and headed for the kitchen. As I set down the groceries on the counter next to the sink, I said, "Kane called me this morning."

"Oh yeah? Just to talk or what?"

"Seemed like it. I'll call him back a little later. I have to think he's bored just sitting behind a desk."

"Ah, he knew the job he was taking. How is Callie doing?" Karen asked. "She has to be due any day now."

"We only talked for a minute. I had to get off the phone. The navigation in the car was acting weird again."

"I'll make an appointment at the dealer," Karen said.

"Or I could just get a different car," I said. "I'm kind of sick of the Pinkmobile."

"It was thousands off because of the color. It was a smart buying decision," Karen said. "But fine, if you want something else, get something else. I was thinking of relinquishing the vehicle-buying decisions to you anyway."

"Really?" I asked. Karen had picked out my last four or five cars. They had all been awful.

"Yeah. Cars are now going to be your department. I kind of think they should be. Don't you?"

"Hell yeah. I'm getting something cool, then. Enough of this slow hybrid crap," I said.

She smiled. "Just settle down. I'm still going to retain veto ability."

"Damn," I said. "Oh, I got made fun of for looking like a stereotypical FBI agent today."

"By who?"

"Coworker. Maybe along with the vehicles rights, I could get clothing rights as well?" I asked.

"Hank, I've seen how you look when you dress yourself. That is still one-hundred-percent my department."

"Fine. You seemed like you were being generous, so I had to throw it out there."

Karen smiled and walked to me. She wrapped her arms around my neck, and I dropped my hands and held her by her waist.

"So," she said. "Don't leave me in suspense. How was your first day? Aside from being made fun of for looking the part."

"We talked on the phone like four times," I said.

She ran her hand along the side of my head, staring at me

with her dark eyes. "I don't care. Tell me again," she said.

"You first."

"Same old same. Make sure everyone is doing their job. Find traffickers, take down traffickers. Okay, now you."

"It was fine. I met the team and got acclimated. Learned some things." I paused. "They gave me my first assignment."

She furrowed her eyebrows. "They put you on something already? You didn't mention that part."

"Yeah, I was waiting to tell you until I was home. I'm going to need to pack tonight. I leave in the morning for Chicago."

Karen snapped her head back. "You're shitting me, right? They are sending you out on something after being there a day. For how long?"

I shrugged. "They didn't mention that part."

"Hank. Look at this place. We're not even settled in, and you have to leave?"

"It's the job, I guess," I said.

She let out a hard breath and dropped her hands from my neck. She walked toward the stairs to head up to the bedroom and spoke over her shoulder. "Okay, well, we're definitely going out, then. I'll help you pack when we get home."

I followed her. "Sure," I said. "Sorry that I have to leave."

"No. I know. It just seems a little rushed to me." Karen reached the top of the stairs and turned left into the master bedroom. She headed to the closet door and pulled it open before unbuttoning her blazer and grabbing a hanger.

I stood in the bedroom doorway and leaned against the

sill. "Trial by fire, or so that's what Ball said. May as well see how I do right out of the gates."

Karen hung her jacket and began looking through her dresses for what I assumed was something to wear out on the town.

"Little black one," I said.

"You think?" she asked, looking over at me.

I nodded.

She pulled the little black one from the hanger and held it up before her. "So are they sending you with someone or the whole team or what?"

"Me and another agent."

She brushed over the front of the dress with the back of her hand. "What's he like? Do you think you'll work well together?"

"Um." I scratched the back of my head. Karen could be a little emotional on certain topics as of late. I figured being sent out of town with another woman could be one of those topics. We were trying to have a child, and she was taking some things to help us with that, one problem being the emotional side effects of the fertility aids the doctor prescribed. I gave her the truth and braced myself. "It's actually a she."

Her head snapped around, and her eyes locked on me. "A she?"

"Yeah."

Karen looked away. "What's her name?"

"Agent Harper." I hoped a title and surname would end the conversation—it didn't.

"What's she like?" Karen asked.

"Seemed professional."

"Oh," Karen said. "Married?"

"Don't know."

She looked over at me and cocked her head to one side. That was a common pose when she wasn't buying what I was selling.

"You didn't look for a ring?" she asked.

"I don't know. Looking for rings on women's fingers isn't really something I do."

She was quiet for a moment. "Well, what does she look like?"

I let out a breath. She wasn't going to quit with her interrogation.

"Is that going to matter for catching a potential serial killer?" I asked.

"I'm just asking."

"I don't know, Karen. Why does it matter?"

"So she's good looking." Karen hung the dress back on the rack.

I rolled my eyes and cracked my neck from side to side. I pulled myself from the doorway and walked over to her. She gave me her back and acted as though she was looking for another dress. I wrapped my arms around her waist and kissed her on the side of the neck. "Do you really think there's a reason for you to be worrying about this?" I asked.

"No," she said.

She turned toward me.

I pulled her in close. "You're the only one for me. Emotional craziness and all."

"Don't make fun of me, Hank. I can't really help it right now."

"I'm not making fun of you. I'm serious. No one else. Ever."

"Promise?" she asked.

"Promise."

"Even if we never have kids?"

"Yup."

She wrapped her arms around me. "Even if I lose a leg?"

I nodded. "I'm not sure why you would, but sure. Your new nickname can be Peggy."

Karen swatted my back with her hand.

"Or Eileen?" I said

Karen pressed her head against my chest and tightened her grip on me—she stayed that way for a minute or so. Then she pulled back. "Okay. Jealous emotions passed. I'm going to go start dinner."

I kissed her on the forehead. "I'll give you a hand."

CHAPTER SIX

Brett had parked Becca's car in line with the others in his outbuilding. The large red shed stood an acre away from the house. He found a dusty old cover to place over it and stacked boxes around and on top of it, just like the vehicle next to it and the vehicle next to that one. To the casual observer, not that there would be anyone stopping over, the cars would have appeared to have been there for years—some had been. With her vehicle parked inside, he was now officially out of space. He'd need to dispose of the vehicles eventually. Brett had been considering burying them on his land.

As he neared Englewood, a southern suburb of Chicago, the time on his Jeep's radio read a few minutes past three o'clock in the morning. Forty miles from home, he clicked on his directional and exited the freeway. Brett drove up and down several blocks, taking in his surroundings. Boarded up homes and businesses lined the streets. He'd heard the reports and seen the articles about deterioration and abundant crime but had never actually stepped foot in that area of town. Brett stopped for a traffic signal. The four-way intersection featured a liquor store with metal barred windows directly across from him. Sitting out front were a group of five or six men. To his right was a small gas station and service shop. A sign out front offered used tires for sale. The light turned green.

Brett cranked the wheel to the left and made his way down the street, watching the random people walking the sidewalks and gathering on porches. He needed a place more remote. He continued up the street for another mile and stopped for another red light. Out his windshield on the left corner of the intersection was an older, rough-looking discount grocery store. Brett looked left to right through the windshield and checked his rearview and side mirrors, spotting no one. The area looked quiet.

Brett turned left when the light turned green and made a right into the back portion of the parking lot. He kept his eyes focused on the top of the building and single light pole but saw no cameras. A moment later, he realized it wouldn't matter as he spotted an Out of Business sign taped to the side doors. Brett weaved through the small parking lot and crept down the alley behind the grocery store. A ten-foot-high wooden fence followed him on the left side of his vehicle, the building on his right. Brett spotted a row of Dumpsters near the back of the alleyway.

He smiled. Brett killed his headlights and pulled the truck all the way to the back of the grocery store. He shut down the motor next to the Dumpsters, took a pair of gloves from the passenger seat, and stepped out. Brett gloved his hands and walked to the closest Dumpster. He flipped the lid up, walked to the back gate of the Jeep, and opened it. Before him was Becca's body, reclothed and wrapped in plastic. Her sunglasses covered her eyes. He folded away the piece of plastic covering her and placed his right hand under her knees and his left under her shoulders. After lifting her from the back of the Jeep, he walked her to the Dumpster and heaved her inside. Her body hit the Dumpster's garbage-covered bottom with a thump. Brett flipped the lid closed and got back in the truck.

CHAPTER SEVEN

"What time does your flight go out?" Karen asked.

"Nine forty-something."

"And this guy is draining people of blood?" she asked.

I nodded. "They have thirteen women attributed to him. Seems like he kills for a month or two and then disappears for years. Eight years ago was the last time he was active. Five bodies turned up in Columbus, Ohio. Before that by a couple of years, the bodies were in St. Louis. Now it's Chicago."

Karen headed for the split between arriving and departing flights. We pulled in and slowed.

She looked over at me. "Just be careful, and no being a goof."

"Goof?" I asked.

"I know how you and Kane were with the constant back and forth," Karen said. "I'm just saying be professional until these new coworkers get to know you."

"Got it," I said. "No being myself."

"That's not what I'm saying."

"I know. I know." I pointed at the airline's entry.

"Right there."

"And don't spread it on about me wearing the pants in our marriage."

I smirked. "Yes, ma'am."

Karen pulled to the curb in the airport's drop zone for departures.

Beth was sitting on a bench beside the sliding entrance doors. I tossed her a wave.

"That's her?" Karen asked.

"Yeah," I said.

"The hot twenty-something-year-old with the doe eyes? You're not serious."

"I think she's a little older than that. Come on. Why don't you see me off and say hi."

"Ugh." Karen shook her head. "Wow, I really sound like a bitch. I'm sorry. I'm blaming the drugs."

I leaned over and gave her a kiss. "I forgive you."

Karen smiled. "I'm glad you have a high tolerance for me. Okay. Best behavior. Here we go."

I laughed and stepped from the passenger side of Karen's truck. I opened the rear door, reached in, and grabbed my suitcase and laptop bag. Karen exited from the other side. She rounded the front and met me on the passenger side. I set my suitcase on the curb, draped my laptop bag over my shoulder, and gave Karen a hug. I looked at Beth and gave her a wave to come over.

"This is my wife, Karen," I said as Beth approached.

"Hi," Karen said. She held out her hand to shake Beth's.

Beth shook her hand and smiled. "Nice to meet you. DEA, right?"

"Yup." Karen released her grip on Beth's hand, which

I was positive was a lot firmer than it ought to be. "Any idea how long you will be keeping my husband away?"

"The less time it takes, the better it is for the bureau. These things never really take longer than a week. They send us out—we see what we can find. If we can't get anywhere on location, we come back and continue from HQ."

Karen nodded. "Okay." Then she looked at me. "Go catch some bad guys, baby." She reached up and rubbed the back of my hair then turned and headed back toward the truck. She looked at me over the truck's hood. "Love you. Call me when you're there."

"Love you, too. I will," I said.

Karen got in and pulled from the curb. Beth and I wheeled our suitcases into the airport.

Beth jabbed me in the ribs with her elbow and whistled as soon as we were inside. "Your wife is hot, Hank."

"Um. Thanks," I said.

"She was nice too. Hell of a handshake."

I just smiled and nodded.

We checked our bags, passed through security, and headed up to our concourse.

"Do you have your case file and everything?" Beth asked.

I patted the side of my laptop bag. "I have everything. So how is this going to go when we get there?"

"We'll pick up our rental cars from the airport and head to the local bureau office. I have the name of the agent that's working the case that we should contact there. We'll check in and see if there have been any updates that we need to be aware of. From there, we'll go to our hotel, get settled, and then get a plan in place for where and how we want to start."

That sounded logical enough.

"Are we working out of the local bureau's office?" I asked.

"I usually don't. They'd obviously supply us with a work area or office if we wanted, but I prefer to just handle everything from the hotel. We'll be on the road most of the time, meeting with people anyway. We'll stop into the local FBI office when we need to."

"Sure," I said.

Our plane boarded within the hour. We sat in business class, side by side. The two-hour flight would have been best served looking over the file, but photos and details of dead bodies wasn't acceptable reading fare in a metal tube filled with a hundred and some people. So Beth and I chatted—mostly small talk. She asked how I liked the area and was adjusting to the move. I told her it was too early to tell. I picked up a little more information on her. She'd been at the FBI for six years, in the homicide division of the serial crimes unit for two. She was originally from the Chicago area, which could come in helpful as far as getting around. Beth was thirty-two. I looked for a ring and didn't spot one.

Our flight landed just before eleven, local time. We picked up our vehicles from the rental-car office and were making our way into the city to the FBI headquarters when I pulled out my phone and called Karen.

She picked up right away. "Made it?" she asked.

"Yeah. I'm in my rental car now, heading for the downtown bureau office. I guess we're meeting with the agent in charge of this investigation and seeing where the local office is at with it."

"And then?" she asked.

"Heading to the hotel. We'll probably figure out where we want to get started on our side of the investigation and go from there."

Beth was merging into the right lane of the freeway, so I put on my turn signal and got behind her.

"Okay. I have a meeting in a couple minutes," Karen said. "Do you want to just call me when you get to the hotel and have a minute later?"

"Yup. That's fine," I said.

"Okay, then I'll talk to you later. Love you."

"Love you too," I said.

She hung up.

Beth exited the freeway, and I followed. Two turns and a half mile of surface streets later, she turned into the FBI headquarters complex. We drove toward the main building and slowed at the gate-guarded entrance. Beth pulled up to the man in the guard shack and passed him her credentials. The gate opened in front of her car, and she passed through. I pulled up and lowered my window.

The guard leaned out from the shack's window. "With the lady?" he asked.

I nodded.

"Just need to see your badge."

I pulled it from my suit pocket and passed it to him. He took it from me and scanned it.

"All set, Agent Rawlings," he said.

I put my badge back in my pocket and pulled through the metal gate. The Agent Rawlings thing was going to take some getting used to.

I found Beth parking in the lot off to my left. I made my way over to her and pulled in my rental alongside hers.

Beth stepped out from her car and grabbed her bag from the back. I killed the motor, grabbed my laptop bag from the passenger seat, and stepped out.

She waved me to her car, and I walked over.

"We'll stop in at the main desk and let them call up to our contact agent," she said. Beth nodded at the large, ten-story white rectangular building with bowed sides. It looked as though it had been constructed fairly recently. What wasn't white on the sides and front was glass. We headed over, and I stared up at the building. The place looked more like an upscale hotel than a government facility. The entrance we walked toward had a courtyard recessed back into the building. A long rectangular flower garden took up the center of the area, and to each side of the flower garden sat benches. As we got closer, I noticed the flower garden and benches actually continued indoors.

"Have you been in here before?" I asked.

"Yeah, it's a neat place," Beth said. "Cool architecture."

"New?" I asked.

"Maybe like ten years old or so." She pointed toward a set of doors to our right. "We're headed over there."

We entered the building's lobby. A number of people rummaged about, all looking hurried. A large FBI insignia was inlaid into the blue marble floor in the center of the room. I followed Beth to the desk at the back.

A man looking the part of a security guard glanced up at us from behind the counter.

"Agents Harper and Rawlings to see an Agent Andrews in serial crimes," Beth said.

"One moment," he said.

The man got on the phone, said that Agent Andrews

had a pair of guests, gave our names, and hung up.

"You'll want to use the elevators there"—he pointed to the corner of the lobby—"and head up to the eighth floor. Make a left out of the elevators and head down the hall to the serial crimes unit. Agent Andrews will be expecting you."

"Thank you," I said.

Beth and I walked to the bank of elevators, and I thumbed the button to take us up.

The elevator doors spread and took us inside. We rode up in silence. The elevator doors opened and let us into a hallway. A sign on the wall showed that the serial crimes unit was to our left, just as the guard downstairs had said. We walked down the hall and entered a large cubicle-filled area that looked strikingly similar to ours in Manassas.

A man in a suit walked toward us. He was six foot and thin and looked to be in his midforties. His hair was short and blond, his face shaved clean. He wore a blue jacket over a light-gray shirt and darker-gray tie. The jacket had FBI embroidered in yellow across the front pocket. He greeted us immediately. "Are you my two from Virginia?" he asked.

"That would be us. Agents Beth Harper and Hank Rawlings," Beth said.

"Agent Alan Andrews," he said.

Beth reached out and shook his hand. I shook the agent's hand next.

"Follow me," he said.

Beth and I followed him around the room of cubicles to an office near the back. He opened the door and motioned for us to sit. We took seats as he closed the door. Agent Andrews rounded his desk and sat. He had a file open on his desk, and though it was upside down, I recognized the photos of one of the victims. "Did you guys get everything we sent over?" he asked.

Beth removed her copy of the file from her bag, so I unzipped my laptop bag and removed mine.

"Here is everything we were given," Beth said. "Have a look and see if we are matching up on everything."

Agent Andrews compared his file against the one Beth had handed him. "Hmm," he said. "Everything you have we have except we never got a few of these crime-scene photos from the first victim that we had. Mind if I make a few copies quick?"

"By all means," Beth said. "After we're contacted for an investigation, our guys pull files from everywhere individually. Those may have come from the PD directly."

He nodded and slipped the four pages into the copy machine at the back of his office.

"We also have this if you'd like to make a copy." Beth slipped out the profile of our suspect, which had been drawn up some eight years before. I had looked it over, but I'd never put a lot of stock in profiles. They all read basically the same—single, possibly divorced thirty-or-forty-something-year-old with a checkered past. I'm sure the bureau's behavior analysis unit would disagree with me on the topic, but I'd been around enough homicides over the years to be entitled to my own opinion.

"Well, the victims were in the Chicago vicinity here. Let's hope our perp still is. You guys have the full force of this office for whatever you need locally," Andrews said.

"Thank you," Beth said.

"Will you be needing an office?" he asked.

Beth shook her head. "No. We'll work from our hotel and coordinate with you on everything."

"Okay," he said.

"What does your gut tell you on these latest victims?" I asked.

Andrews looked at me. "You want my take on it?"

I nodded.

"Well, I looked over what had been put together on this investigation, including the files from the prior homicides. There's a reason behind the draining of blood. What it is, I don't know. It's an odd way to kill someone. I've been looking into that angle. The blood was drained by inserting needles into the main arteries. It's not how a mortician would do it. I want to think that there may be something there, but we came up empty on that front."

"I did a fair amount of research on the same," Beth said. "I didn't get anywhere with it either. As far as I can tell, it's just this guy's method of killing."

"Same thing I was thinking," Andrews said. "The stomach contents from the autopsy reports are all the same with these latest victims. Alcohol and some kind of bow-tie pasta that's barely digested, meaning they were killed shortly after eating."

Beth nodded. "These victims trust this guy. It's the only way he could get away with drugging them. There's too much Rohypnol for this to be in a public setting, meaning they have to be alone with him somewhere. And if it's the same food, that means he's cooking it."

I nodded, agreeing. "How hard did you guys dig into each woman's personal life?" I asked.

"We worked it. There's nothing that really sticks out. We pulled bank records, phone records, e-mails."

"And nothing at all?" I asked. "No cell-phone GPS tracking?"

"Nope. The only cell phone we found was Jasmine Thomas's, and it was completely dead. We have our tech team looking into it, but so far, we can't do anything with it."

"What do you mean dead?" I asked. "Like dropped in water?"

"We don't know. It doesn't function. It's going to have to be disassembled and gone through," Andrews said.

"What about ping triangulation to get a general area? Common places the signal pinged from? Anything like that?"

He shook his head. "We requested the records from the phone carriers, which should be here tomorrow morning. The last pings, from the people we've spoken with at the carriers, all show towers near the women's residences or workplaces."

"Okay, as far as last seens or spoken withs on these women?" I asked.

"The two most recent were seen the day of them going missing. The one from a month back had spoken with a family member a few days prior."

"What about vehicles?" I asked.

"Angela Wormack's was at her house, and Jasmine Thomas's was found at her apartment complex. We never found the vehicle of Kennedy Taylor."

I wrote down the information.

"Anything as far as video from places near the body-dump sites?" Beth asked.

Agent Andrews shook his head. "Nothing."

CHAPTER EIGHT

Before leaving the federal building, we spent another hour discussing the local FBI's portion of the investigation, and I took notes. As far as hard evidence went, we didn't get much more than what was in our file. However, I felt that both hearing what they'd already looked into and knowing Agent Andrews's thoughts on the investigation could help.

I followed Beth, driving through downtown Chicago, to our hotel—a half-hour drive from the FBI building.

Beth made a right off north Michigan Avenue, drove around the block to east Walton, and pulled into a valet area under a massive, ornate awning hanging out over the sidewalk of an old building. I pulled in behind her and glanced to my right. Old English lettering on the front of the building read The Drake.

I saw Beth stepping from her car and getting her suitcase and bag from within. She waited under the awning while the valet pulled away with her car and I pulled up. I got out, grabbed my bags, took my ticket, and headed inside with Beth. We left our bags with the bellman and walked up the double flight of stairs to the building's lobby.

Crystal chandeliers hung from the coffered wooden ceiling. Blue carpet with gold patterns covered the floor. A circular table with a huge floral arrangement filled the center of the room. Miscellaneous chairs for lounging and talking were grouped in pairs. I didn't see a single television or computer monitor anywhere. The building was old and extremely elegant. Beth continued walking. She appeared to know where she was going. I followed her toward the hotel's check-in area.

"Been here before?" I asked.

She nodded. "Yup. This hotel is so beautiful. I actually got married here." She continued walking.

Maybe she just didn't wear her ring on the job. "I didn't know you were married," I said.

Beth continued, "Divorced. The marriage only lasted like two weeks. Well, it was more like two years, but it went pretty quick."

I didn't question the topic further but remained quiet.

Beth stopped at the unmanned check-in counter, and I stood to her side.

She looked at me. "He and I are still close."

I nodded. "So how far are we from the sites of the body dumps?"

"Um, from here, the most recent is about a half-hour drive south. The others are about twenty minutes in each direction. We're pretty centrally located between everything."

A woman approached the counter from a room in the back, and we checked in. The woman told us someone would bring our bags up to our rooms. We headed to the elevators, and I thumbed the button to take us up. We stepped off the elevator on the tenth floor and found our rooms down the hall.

Beth stood at her door. "I need to call Ball and give him an update. Then I'm going to get settled in and unpack as soon as my bag comes. I'll pop over in a bit, and we can get started on some things."

"Yeah, sounds fine." I swiped my card in my door and entered the room. The door swung closed at my back.

I walked in farther and took in my surroundings. To my right was a single king-size bed, nightstands to its sides. A wingback chair and a small table stood directly in front of me. To my left was a television sitting on a four-door wood cabinet. A black folder containing the hotel's in-room menu stood beside the television. I pulled the two larger center doors of the television cabinet open. One side was stocked with chips, booze, wine, and snacks. The other side was a mini refrigerator stocked with beer, soda, and champagne. I debated eating some of the chips and snacks—breakfast had been my last meal. I searched the small pamphlet for the prices of the items and flipped it closed when I saw a six-dollar candy bar.

I closed the cabinet doors and crossed the bluish-gray octagon-patterned carpet to the small desk and office chair in the corner near the bed. I set my laptop bag on the desk and removed my suit jacket. I hung my jacket on the back of the chair and went on to check out the bathroom. I reached inside and flipped on the light. Beige marble tiles filled the shower and tub area, and the vanity was topped with a matching marble slab. Decorative wallpaper covered the walls. I flipped the light off and took a seat at the desk. I spun on the chair and looked over the room again. All the furniture in the room was classically designed. It went with the hotel's character of being extremely high end for the last hundred or so years.

I pulled my phone and dialed Karen, but my call went to her voice mail. I left a message that I was at the hotel and would try her back later in the evening. Then I turned back to the desk and removed my computer and the investigation file from my bag. After plugging my computer in, I powered it up and plugged it into my phone to get a secure Internet connection. Then I rocked back in my chair and began looking over the file for a place to start. I opened a search on my computer and plugged in the three most recent victims' names together. I got a handful of news articles and videos mentioning the homicides—that wasn't what I was looking for, but I took a few minutes to read what the local press was reporting. A knock came at the door.

I headed over and pulled the door open. A bellman dressed in a black uniform with a single gold stripe down the center delivered my suitcase. I fished a tip from my wallet, took the bag, thanked him, and closed the door. Then I heaved the suitcase onto the edge of the bed, opened it, and laid out the contents. My underclothes found the drawers of the cabinets, and my suits hung in the closet.

I sat at the desk and thumbed back through the file to the friends-and-family interviews and glanced over the answers for where the victims had been seen last. I shook my head. Someone else's notes in a file wasn't doing it for me. I wanted to contact all the victims' friends and family myself so I could hear the information first hand, so I jotted that down in my notepad. I also wanted to see the scenes where the bodies had been found, interview the people who found them, and talk to the officers that worked those scenes. My to-do list grew.

I heard another knock at the door, so I set my pen down and answered it.

Agent Harper didn't enter. "Hungry?" she asked.

"Starving."

"Let's go get something to eat and spitball how we are proceeding. There's a pretty good burger joint within walking distance if it's still there."

"That works for me." I noticed she didn't have a file or anything other than a small handbag with her, so I grabbed my suit jacket, dropped the file on the table, and left my room.

The restaurant she spoke of wasn't even a full block away. The hostess took us to a booth next to a giant American flag that made up an entire wall. I looked at the plates of the customers eating as we made our way to sit. I saw everything from waffles to shrimp to burgers.

I grabbed a menu and flipped it open. "I want to interview everyone," I said. "Family, friends, officers, the people who found the bodies."

"I agree, and it's needed," she said. "We could split it up, do what we can over the phone—make trips to those that we have to."

"I'm going to get started on making the calls when we get back—get some interviews set to meet people within the next day or two. I think something was overlooked somewhere," I said. "Or the dots not connected somewhere."

Our waitress walked over and introduced herself. I ordered a Philly cheesesteak sandwich, fries, and a soda. Beth got some kind of a salad and an iced tea. The woman left to put in the order.

"What makes you so sure they missed something?" Beth asked. She brushed her brown hair away from the side of her face.

"Call it a hunch. Plus, like you said yesterday. When someone dumps a bunch of bodies in a short time in the same area, they have a good chance of getting caught."

"You were listening."

"Always. If our killer was courting these women, someone had to know about a particular man that their friends or loved ones were seeing. There has to be something that we should be able to match up. A phone number, an e-mail address, a website, something."

"You'd think," Beth said. "It doesn't always work that way, though."

CHAPTER NINE

Brett sat in front of his computer at the desk in his home office, a chat window open on the screen, awaiting a response. His cell phone, sitting on the desk next to a glass and bottle of whiskey, rang. He reached for the phone and looked at the caller ID.

Cracking his knuckles, he leaned back in his wide leather office chair. Then he clicked the button on his phone to answer.

"Hey, Carrie," he said.

"I have your schedule of meetings for tomorrow."

"Sure. What's on the books?"

"We have that meeting set with the media agency and the board to start running the television spots in the morning. That's at nine. Then your eleven o'clock is with a reporter looking to do a human-interest piece. After lunch, you have an appointment at two o'clock with a rep from an energy-drink company that would like to do some sponsored events. The last of the day is at four o'clock with Bill Simms."

"What did Bill want?" Brett asked.

"Um, I think that he received something from your ex-wife's attorney."

Brett let out a puff of air in frustration. "Okay, Carrie. I'll see you in the morning."

"Sure, have a good evening, sir."

Brett hung up. Grumbling, he dialed his ex-wife. The phone rang in his ear and clicked as someone answered.

"So it takes a letter to your attorney to get you to call me back?" she asked.

"I haven't seen the letter. What do you want?" Brett asked.

"What do you mean what do I want? I want my money. I've been trying to call you for weeks."

"Your money? Don't you mean my money, Nicky?"

"Whatever. You're a month behind. It's unacceptable."

Brett scoffed. "Unacceptable?"

"You married me. We had a kid. We got a divorce. You have to pay."

Brett rubbed his eyes. "Yeah, a bunch of bad decisions in a row."

"Well, I also didn't know I was marrying a complete psycho, so it goes both ways."

"Maybe someday I'll get to show you what a complete psycho looks like, Nicky."

"Yeah, well I should have sent your ass to jail about ten different times."

Brett said nothing.

"Whatever. I'm not getting into this with you for the thousandth time. It's called alimony and child support. And it's court ordered," she said. "Just pay it. If I don't see the money in my account by Friday, I'll have my attorney put together the paperwork to have your income garnished."

"You're going to get my income garnished? Good luck with that. You know, I've been thinking about putting a dream team of attorneys together, maybe getting a private eye to follow you around and see what you do. Maybe it's time for that. Maybe I should fight you for custody."

"Stop with the stupid threats and just pay me," she said. "You don't give a shit about Travis and don't want him anyway. It's been over a year since you even spoke to him. You don't even try to call."

"You made it clear that you don't want me as part of his life."

"I just don't want you spending time with him. That doesn't mean you can't call."

"What's the difference?"

"There's something wrong with you. Whatever the hell it is, I don't want it rubbing off on our son. Phone calls are fine. In person, unsupervised, no."

"I'll pay when I see him."

"Not a chance. God. This is so stupid. Just pay the damn money. It's not like it even affects you. What are you making now, like a gazillion dollars a month?"

Brett spoke through a clenched jaw. "It doesn't matter what I make. I give you twenty thousand dollars a month for no damn reason other than I was stupid enough to get you pregnant and then try to do the right thing by marrying you."

"You know what? Screw it. You can deal with my attorney," she said.

Brett heard a dial tone in his ear. He tossed the phone back onto the desk, took the glass of whiskey in his hand, and took a drink.

Shaking his head, Brett thought about Nicky. He'd

only married her to try to appear normal. No one ever suspects the married man with a kid. Yet Brett quickly realized it limited his ability to move about freely. Nicky was always watching. He should have just killed her as he'd planned to all those years before, yet it would have caused immediate suspicion. Brett knew it would get him caught somehow—he was successful in his hobby, he enjoyed it, and he wouldn't risk capture. However, when they were still together, he got tastes of what he desired without Nicky's knowledge.

Brett leaned forward, minimized that chat window, and logged into his online banking. He transferred the funds to Nicky. Brett logged off.

In the drawer of the desk was a ledger with an old beat-up leather cover. Brett removed the book and opened the cover. Every foul, derogatory word he could come up with over the course of eight years littered the pages corners. Doodles of a dead woman scattered the pages as he thumbed through toward the back. Drawings of dollar signs were present on each margin. Brett ran the pen tip down the page and found the blank line below the last entry. He entered her amount—a bit over twenty thousand. He added it to the total—two million twenty-one thousand eighteen dollars and twelve cents since the divorce, a bit over eight years prior.

Brett took a large mouthful of whiskey and swallowed. The chat window popped back up with an incoming message.

He smiled and moved his computer mouse on the screen to view the message—it came from Monica, a woman he'd been in contact with over the last week and a half. He'd met her for lunch earlier in the day.

The message read: *Sorry, I couldn't respond sooner. Yes, I'd love to meet for dinner. Eight is fine. Where should I meet you?*

Brett messaged back: *No problem. How about I send a car to pick you up from your place?*

Monica responded right away: *Send a car?*

Brett responded: *Yeah, I'll have my driver collect you.*

Monica messaged back: *Lol. Collect me, huh? Sure, that's fine.* She included her address at the end of the message.

Brett typed: *Great. Henry, my driver, will be there at 8. Wear something nice. I'll make some reservations.*

Monica responded: *Sounds good, see you later.*

Brett closed the chat window as a smile overtook his face.

He glanced down at his watch. He had a few hours before he would go and pick her up—Henry, the driver, didn't exist. Brett planned to make an excuse that he was in the area and to pick Monica up himself. He would say that he had to stop in at the house quickly because he'd forgotten his wallet or phone or something needed. He would make up a reason to stay there—just as with women past.

Brett wiggled the computer mouse and logged into the master system for the website that he'd been chatting with Monica through. He sent off the virus that would kill her cell phone. It would start by shutting down the phone's signal then move on to its internal and external memory, if so equipped, before killing the main board. He began the process of completely deleting every correspondence she'd ever had from the servers, and something caught his eye.

"Interesting," Brett said.

He dismissed what he'd seen and continued deleting messages. If she used the website through her home computer again, everything would be gone. By design, the pages he used for hunting women on his website didn't save in the browsing history of their computers. All the actions were tedious but necessary to ensure he couldn't be tracked down.

CHAPTER TEN

I clicked End on my cell phone and finished writing the notes I needed in my notepad. Beth was finishing a phone call behind me. I turned my office chair around and faced her. She was sitting in the wingback chair in my room, using the small table beside it as a base to write notes. She thanked whoever she was speaking with and clicked off from the phone call.

Beth adjusted herself in the chair, put one leg up over her other knee, and placed her notepad on her lap.

"Well?" she asked.

"I just finished with Hilary Wormack, the mother of the first victim, Angela Wormack," I said.

"And, anything?"

"She said she last spoke to Angela two days prior to her body being found. One day prior, she made repeated phone calls to her daughter but never received an answer. She said the phone started going straight to voice mail about midway through the day."

"Okay. That lines up with what we had. The going-straight-to-voice-mail part midway through the day could mean that our killer already had her. Was the woman at work, or could anyone physically verify her whereabouts later in the day?" Beth asked.

"The mother said Angela was self-employed. I guess she did freelance graphic-artist work."

"Did she live in an apartment complex or home? Maybe a neighbor saw her?"

I shook my head. "Condo complex. The local PD did some door knocking. Got nothing. As far as what they found, no one had seen the woman for days. The last person who saw her was a friend who went out to a club with her the prior weekend."

"Did you speak with the friend?"

"I did. She was the first I called after the local PD. The woman wasn't much help. She said that Angela was kind of a homebody and she had to persuade her out of the house the prior weekend when they went out. They didn't meet anyone and ended up going home around midnight."

"Nothing seemed off from any stories you got with the mother, friend, et cetera?"

"No. Her mother claimed that she didn't make a lot of money, so she tried to limit what she did, spendingwise."

Beth looked thoughtful. "So if you're a graphic artist and spend most of your time on a computer, I'm betting you spend a fair amount of time online—looking at things, social media, whatever."

"If it's always in front of you and you have nothing better to do, sure."

"We should get her computer for a look," Beth said.

"Not a bad idea. I'll call her mother back to see what became of it. Maybe she'll make it available to us. Her mother, Hilary, can't meet with us until Friday, though. As far as the local PD, the patrol captain I spoke with in district four, where she was found, said we could come tonight. The night shift starts at seven, and he said he would be able to send us out with the two officers that were first on the scene. I didn't give him an exact time that we'd be there. I figured I'd see where we're at with the victim's friends and family first. Aside from that, I called the local medical examiner's office that handled Kennedy Taylor's body. It was after hours, so I left a message. I just wanted to see if her remains were still there and check if we could get a viewing. What about you? What did you get?" I asked.

Beth ran her finger down the notepad in her lap. "We have an interview tomorrow at three o'clock p.m. with Kennedy Taylor's family. It looks like their home is about forty-five minutes from here. I spoke with her father. I guess they are doing some kind of gathering, so their other daughter, who the father said was extremely close with Kennedy, will be there as well. As far as the other victim, we have three numbers for father, mother, and best friend of Jasmine Thomas, our second-to-last victim. I called all three, got three voice mails, and left three messages."

"Okay." I jotted down the interview time in my notepad and looked at my watch—a couple minutes after six. "What did you get with the local PD about seeing the other dump sites?"

"We're set to view the two that happened in the sixteenth district tomorrow evening at eight. The patrol sergeant said he would have someone escort us."

I nodded. "Well, it looks like we're just about set on appointments with everyone except those close with Jasmine Thomas. Are you ready to head over to view the dump site?"

"Sure," Beth said.

"Okay, I'll call the patrol captain back and let him know we're on our way."

"I'll call for the car," Beth said.

I dialed the patrol captain, confirmed that we'd be there within the hour, and hung up. I stuffed my notepad and pen in the pocket of my suit jacket hanging over the back of my office chair. Then I stood and pulled my jacket on.

"Ready?" she asked.

"Ready as I'll get."

She headed for the door, and I followed.

The valet out front of the hotel had her car waiting when we stepped from the front doors. I handed the guy a tip and hopped in the passenger side. Beth took a seat behind the wheel and looked over at me. "You don't want to drive?"

"I didn't think about it," I said.

"Did you want to?"

"Nope. You're fine. I guess I'm used to riding shotgun when I'm on duty."

"Old partner always drove, huh?"

"Technically, he was my boss," I said, "but yeah, he drove more often than not."

Beth shifted into drive and pulled from the front of the hotel. She put on her directional to make a left at the lights. "So he was what? A lieutenant?"

"He was a lieutenant. He's the captain of Tampa homicide now."

"What was he like?"

"What was he like?" I thought for a moment. "I don't know. It's kind of hard to jam years working daily with someone into a few words. Um. Put it this way, aside from being a damn good cop, I could call the guy from any place in the world, at any time, and he'd be there to help."

"Can't really ask for more than that," she said.

"What's it like being out in the field with Bill and Scott?" I asked. "I assume you've worked investigations with them like we are now."

"Yeah, I've been in the field with both Bill and Scott a handful of times each. Ah, it's kind of hard to describe, for me. When they go out together on an investigation, they come back with stories and such. I'm not sure what the bond that partners have is called."

"Friendship, maybe," I said.

"More like brothers. I guess I don't really see that when I'm out with them. It's basically do your job and head back. And then that's the end of it. Maybe it's because I'm a woman."

I didn't really have any insight to provide, so I remained quiet. I definitely didn't want to get into a conversation about how I felt about working with her— we hadn't spent enough time together, and any answer I provided would probably be taken the wrong way.

"I'm okay to work with so far, right?" she asked.

Shit.

I needed to answer fast. "Yeah, sure," I said. "Hell, you're showing me the ropes. It's appreciated."

"Well, I think you're doing fine so far. I'll make sure I give you a good report. Ball wanted me to evaluate how you did out here."

I hadn't known I was under evaluation, but that made sense, it being my first investigation and all. "Damn well going to do my best," I said.

She nodded. "I'm sure you will. Yeah, the last guy we brought into the team didn't do so hot in the field. Ball, unfortunately, had to let him go after his first investigation."

"Oh," I said. "Who did he go out in the field with?" I looked over at her.

Beth's eyes didn't leave the road in front of her. "Me," she said.

I nodded but didn't respond.

"Yeah, he didn't really do anything wrong, per se, and we actually caught the guy, but he just didn't seem like a good fit to the team. So I let Ball know, and he kicked him loose. I kind of felt bad about it. I mean, the guy moved here from out west. He had a couple of young children. I think his wife was in poor health. It just didn't work."

I looked over at Beth again and furrowed my brow. She was laying the story on pretty thick. Beth was looking out the driver's side window. I caught her reflection smiling in the glass. She was bullshitting me as I expected from her last few comments.

"Sure. You have to be able to work well with your coworkers," I said. "So the report thing... is that the sheet that Ball gave me that said Peer Evaluation at the top? I just glanced at it before I left Monday, but it looked like I was supposed to fill out what I thought of working with you."

Her head snapped toward me. "Peer evaluation sheet?" she asked.

I shrugged. "Yeah, I don't know. It looked like some kind of official form. It had your name on it and a bunch of questions."

"And Ball gave it to you?" she asked.

"Yeah. He just said, 'Fill this out after you're through.'"

She said nothing.

I gave her a second to stew.

"I was actually kidding about the report and whole coworker getting let go thing," she said.

"Yeah, I know," I said.

"You know?"

"Yeah, I saw your reflection in the driver's window. Try not to smile when you're feeding me b.s."

"Oh, you're a jerk," she said.

CHAPTER ELEVEN

We made a brief stop at the police station, met with a pair of officers that had worked the crime scene, and headed out. Beth and I followed Officers Murray and Nelson in their marked patrol cruiser to where Angela Wormack's body had been found. The patrol car pulled to the side of the street in front of a two-story dark-brown home and turned in to a fenced-in parking lot on our right, which separated the home and a tavern. We pulled in behind the officers' car and found a spot. I checked the time—we were right at 7:30 p.m.

Beth shut off the car, and we stepped out. I surveyed our surroundings. The tavern's front entrance was directly before us. Next to the tavern was an insurance office, its entrance also facing the parking lot. I glanced to my right. The brown home we'd passed turning in sat horizontally to the parking lot while the garage off the back faced the lot. Farther down were another business and a duplex, both facing the parking lot.

"Kind of a weird arrangement," I said.

"Yeah, with houses and businesses sharing a common

center parking lot," she said.

The two patrol officers stepped out of their cruiser. The driver, Nelson, was early thirties and looked as though he'd spent years in the gym. He wore a police-issue mustache and a dark-brown buzz cut. The passenger, Murray, looked to be late twenties and almost as fit as his partner. He was clean shaven, a set of dark sunglasses hiding his eyes. Both men wore Chicago PD uniforms consisting of a dark-blue tactical vest over a light-blue button-up shirt. Each man wore a Chicago PD baseball hat with a badge and checkered stripe embroidered on the front.

"Dumpster back by the Winnebago," Nelson said. He jerked his chin toward an RV parked next to the duplex near the back of the parking lot.

The two patrol officers walked toward the Dumpster, and Beth and I followed.

The nineteen-seventies RV was a cream color with a tan bottom. An orange-and-yellow stripe ran down the side, forming a W at the front. On the far side of the RV sat a single green Dumpster. We approached.

"We were first on the scene," Murray said. He pulled his sunglasses from his eyes and slipped them into the breast pocket of his tactical vest. "Right before our shift ended. Maybe fifteen minutes or so."

"What time is that?" Beth asked.

"Shift ends at seven a.m., so six forty-five," Nelson answered. "We got the call that someone found a body in the Dumpster. Arrived to the scene and met with the caller. Lives in the right side of the blue duplex there." He pointed over to the home. "The guy says he was taking out the trash before work and saw the woman inside. He walks us over, and we confirm, in fact, that there is a deceased woman inside."

"We called in our forensics team. They dusted the Dumpster and dug through what little contents were inside. Got nothing though," Murray said.

"And none of the residents that live in the houses here"—I pointed—"or the business owners saw anything?"

"This is kind of its own contained area here. We spoke with each resident and business owner. Nobody saw anything," Murray said.

"We even stopped in here around bar close the following night and asked the patrons and staff if they'd seen anything going on over here the night prior," Nelson said. "Nothing."

"No video in this lot anywhere?" Beth asked.

Neither replied but both shook their heads.

"We got into contact with the company that services the Dumpster. Their guy was here around ten a.m. the day prior to the resident finding the body. So we have about a twenty-hour window of when she could have been put in there. We thought we'd be able to trim that time frame down a bit when our guys dug through the couple bags of trash that were inside and found out which home it came from." Nelson pointed at the brown house facing the street. "We asked when they'd tossed it. The guy said he had his kid take it out around dinner time, five o'clock or so. It didn't really help us out. The kid was too short to see inside. He wouldn't have noticed if there was a body in there or not," Nelson said.

"So, body, no one saw anything, and no evidence left behind," Beth said.

Nelson removed his hat and wiped his sleeved bicep across his forehead. He put the baseball cap back on his head and snugged it down. "That's about the extent of it," he said. "We obviously didn't know that we were dealing with some kind of serial killer. It was just a woman, dead, in a Dumpster. She didn't even look injured."

Beth nodded.

Something caught my attention from the corner of my eye. I looked at the Winnebago. The sun-faded curtain in one of the side windows of the RV moved. "You guys ever check the RV here?" I asked.

The two patrol officers looked at each other.

"Um, no, I don't think so," Nelson said.

"It looks like someone is inside of it," I said.

"In that old heap?" Murray asked. "That thing looks like it's been sitting there for ten years."

"Could be," I said. "Could also be someone living in it."

I walked to the RV's side door and rapped my knuckles on the metal. I heard footsteps inside but didn't receive an answer at the door, so I banged my fist on it again. "FBI, open up."

That was the first time I'd announced myself as such—the phrase didn't yet sound natural in my ears. A moment later, the doorknob turned, and the door pushed open. A large, overweight man appearing in his sixties stood in the doorway in his underwear. Gray hair covered his chest, belly, and legs. His head was bald. A white beard took up space on his chin. In his right hand was a beer in a Chicago Bears koozie, in his left hand, a cigarette.

"Help you?" he asked.

I flipped open my bifold and showed him my FBI

badge. "Agent Rawlings with the FBI. I have a couple questions. Mind putting on some pants for me, sir?" I said.

"I'm in my house. I'll damn well stand here in my underwear if I want."

I shrugged and stuffed my credentials back in my suit jacket. "Whatever. Do you live in this vehicle?" I asked.

"Yeah, and I pay to park here. So what of it?"

Beth took up a spot to my side and looked through the doorway at the man.

"Mind putting some pants on for me, please?" she asked.

"What's the matter, princess?" He took a pull from his cigarette. "You don't like the view?" he asked.

"Pants." Beth snapped her fingers. "Now, or I'll find something we can arrest you for. I don't think you'll be a fan of the Cook County Jail, arriving like that. Some people there might be fans of you, though if this is how you're taken in."

"Ugh, fine." The man disappeared from the doorway.

I looked at Beth.

She shrugged and ran a hand through her dark hair. "What? I don't want to stand here and stare at his hairy gut."

I smirked.

He came back to the doorway a moment later in some orange-striped sweatpants and a T-shirt. "What do you two want, anyway?"

"Did you see or hear anything going on over by this Dumpster maybe a month or so ago?" I asked.

"I assume you're talking about the body they fished out of there?"

"Yeah," I said.

"I can't be sure," he said. "Which is why I didn't bother talking to the cops that were here."

"Why don't you tell us what you're not sure about," Beth said.

"Well, I got woken up by a noise late the night prior to the cops digging around. Or early that morning, depending how you're looking at it. It sounded like someone dumping something in the Dumpster. Well, it was either that or raccoons. I didn't get up to look."

"What time was this?" I asked.

"Maybe about four in the morning." He lifted one arm and scratched at his exposed armpit with his other hand, holding the beer. "Might have been a few minutes after that. I don't know. Middle of the night."

"And you didn't get up to look?" Beth asked.

"No. Why would I get out of bed to watch someone throwing out the trash in the middle of the night?"

The guy did have a point.

"Other than what you heard, anything else?" I asked. "See any strange people or cars that weren't normally around here?"

He shrugged. "We have a bar in the lot. Different cars in and out of here every day and night."

My cell phone vibrated against my leg in my pocket. I slipped the phone out and looked at the screen but didn't recognize the number.

I excused myself from Beth and the man then answered the call. "Agent Rawlings."

"Mark Green, Cook County night shift medical examiner. I got your message regarding the remains of Kennedy Taylor."

"Yes, hello. I'd like to view the body if possible."

"Well, it's already gone from our facility. We released the remains to a crematorium yesterday at the family's request."

"Any idea if the remains have actually been cremated?" I asked.

"No idea. Not much to see there either way, aside from a few needle marks. We could give you the results from the autopsy if that helps."

"I already have it. I guess I was just looking for a little personal insight into the remains."

"The body was drained of blood. Needle marks in arms, legs, and neck. Tox screen showed Rohypnol."

"That much I know. Nothing else stood out?" I asked.

"Not really. Stomach contents—"

I cut him off. "Contained alcohol and some kind of pasta that was barely digested."

"Yeah. Exactly. How did you know that?"

I told him the stomach contents had been the same with previous victims. We spoke for another few minutes, but he didn't have anything else for me. I hung up and walked back to Beth. The door on the Winnebago was closed, and she was standing with the two officers.

"Done with underwear guy?" I asked.

"Yeah, he doesn't know anything. Who was on the phone?" she asked.

"Medical examiner that handled Kennedy Taylor."

"And?"

"The body was already sent over for cremation. Nothing new."

Beth and I thanked the patrol officers for meeting us and headed back for the hotel. We pulled up to the valet at the front entrance a bit before nine o'clock. Beth and I had put in a full day plus with the traveling. We walked through the front entrance and climbed the stairs toward the lobby. Beth stopped halfway up the flight of steps and dug her hand into the front pocket of her blazer. She pulled her phone out and hit the button to talk.

"Agent Beth Harper," she said.

I continued up the flight of steps to take a seat in the lobby and wait for her to finish her call. She met me a moment later.

"That was the mother of Jasmine Thomas, our second-most-recent victim. We have an appointment with her tomorrow morning at ten."

"Good," I said.

"That's enough for the night," Beth said. She motioned toward the elevators. We walked over, and she thumbed the button to take us upstairs.

I dug my fingers into my eyes and gave them a hard rub. The elevator doors opened, took us inside, and let us out on the tenth floor a moment later. Beth and I walked for our rooms. I fished my hotel key card from my wallet.

Beth looked over at me from her room door. "Are you going to sleep soon?" she asked.

"I don't know. I'll probably call my wife, relax in front of the television for a bit, and call it a night."

"Feel like going downstairs and getting a drink?" she asked.

I took a rain check.

CHAPTER TWELVE

Brett pulled the Ferrari past the front door of the address Monica had given him.

"Shit," he said.

Her apartment complex was above a row of cafes and small businesses. People roamed the sidewalks back and forth. The stairs leading to the entrance of her building were immediately to the right of the cafes' outdoor seating—seating that appeared full. Brett continued for a block or two and found a parking spot on a side street. He parked, placed a baseball cap upon his head, and stepped from his car. Then he walked back to her building.

He kept his head down and to the right as he passed the cafe. Brett quickly climbed the stairs and walked through the glass door of Monica's building. He stood in a small entryway the size of a closet. Another door, which was locked, led into the apartment building itself. Before Brett was a row of buttons on the wall to buzz each apartment. He found her name next to unit three eighteen. He thumbed down the button.

"Hello," a woman's voice called.

"Here to pick you up," he said.

"Sure, I'll be down in a minute."

Brett waited in the entryway. A moment later, he saw her approaching from an elevator down the hall.

She opened the locked door. "Oh, it's you. I thought you were sending a driver."

"I couldn't get a hold of him, so I figured I'd pick you up myself. I tried sending you a message, but I never got a response," Brett said.

"Yeah, my phone just up and died. Weirdest thing. I went to grab it to make a call, and it just did nothing. I swapped batteries, everything. Whatever. I guess I'll have to get a new one tomorrow on my lunch break."

"Yeah, that's definitely odd. You didn't get it wet, did you?" Brett asked.

"No, not at all."

"Well, more bad news. I was in a rush out the door and forgot my wallet, so we'll have to stop and get it." Brett looked down at his watch. "We have like an hour and a half until our dinner reservation, so we should be fine."

"Oh, okay," Monica said.

Brett looked her up and down. She wore a tight white dress with thin straps at the top.

"You look amazing," he said.

"Thanks. You don't look so bad yourself," she said.

Brett smirked but said nothing. He was wearing a black tailored suit. His shoes were a couple thousand—his watch more. The amount of scruff on his cheeks was perfect. He waved for her to follow him out from the building's entryway.

She did.

"Where's your car?" she asked.

"I had to park like two blocks away. I drove past and couldn't find a single spot, but now there are a bunch."

She shook her head. "A lot of weird stuff seems to be going on. Maybe it's a sign."

Brett chuckled. "Yeah, maybe." He walked fast past the cafe, trying to get off of her heavily populated block as quickly as possible.

"Where's the fire?" she asked. Monica jogged a couple steps in her high heels to catch up to him.

"Oh, sorry." He slowed and let her meet him at his side as he placed his hand at the small of her back. "I didn't have any change, so I didn't put anything in the parking meter. I don't want to get a ticket."

Brett crossed the street, and the pair found his car and got in.

"Wow, Rick. I've never been in one of these. I saw the photos of it online in your ad. This thing is so cool."

"Yeah." He fired the motor and revved the engine. "A little pricey." He chuckled. "I actually have a more expensive one on the way." That was a lie.

"Wow," she said again. "I can't imagine what a car payment on something like this would be."

"No car payment," Brett said. "Just a purchase."

He quickly glanced over to catch her reaction. She looked at him and smiled.

Monica reached over and placed her hand on his thigh. "How far away is your house?"

"About a half hour. We'll still be able to make our reservations, and if we don't, I'm sure the restaurant will accommodate us. I'm friends with the owner."

"Oh, okay," she said.

Brett smirked—he had no reservations at any

restaurant. He exchanged a bit of small talk with the woman on the drive toward his house—it mostly consisted of her talking about her phone and him talking over her head about business.

Brett pulled up to the front gates at his driveway.

"This is your place?" Monica asked.

Brett reached from the window of his car and punched in the gate code. "One of them. I have another home in St. Louis and another outside of Columbus. My business has a regional office in each location. I also have a condo in Aspen."

"I don't know if you ever actually told me what you do."

"Oh, actually, I own the site you found me on."

She jerked her head back. "What? You own Classified OD?"

Brett smiled and nodded.

The gates spread. Brett drove up the driveway and stopped just beyond the front of the home. He shut the car off and stepped out while Monica remained in the car. He pretended he was receiving a phone call, putting the phone to his ear. After a few seconds, he walked to the passenger side and opened her door.

"That was my driver," he said. "He's going to meet us here and pick us up. He should be here in about a half hour. Care for a tour while we wait?"

"Okay, sure."

Monica stepped out and looked around, staring at the brick home. "Wow, Rick. This place is great."

"Thanks. I wanted a place with a fair amount of land. When this place came on the market, listed with twenty-some acres, I kind of fell in love with it."

Brett walked toward the front door, and Monica followed. He unlocked it and entered.

"Glass of wine while we wait?" he asked.

"Yeah, that would be fine," she said.

"I just got this new bottle from France that's supposed to be to die for. We'll have a glass, walk around the house and grounds for a bit, and then take off when Henry gets here."

"Sounds good," she said.

"Make yourself at home." Brett pointed toward the living room. "I'll bring you a glass."

"Thanks," she said.

Brett went to the kitchen and pulled open the drawer beside the refrigerator. He removed a small Tupperware dish of powdered Rohypnol. The drug had been in pill form when he acquired it in Mexico years prior—grinding it into a powder made dissolving it into a food or drink much easier. He took the lid off the dish—inside was a plastic teaspoon. Brett grabbed a pair of wine glasses from the cupboard and a bottle of wine from the rack on the counter. He turned the bottle in his hand and looked at the label. The wine was some everyday brand he'd picked up for a few dollars at the grocery store.

Brett scooped a teaspoon of the Rohypnol from the container and placed it in one of the glasses. He uncorked the bottle and poured wine over the top of the powder to dissolve it. With a few swirls of the wine in the glass, the powder remaining at the bottom dissolved. Brett filled his glass and walked from the kitchen back to the woman. He handed the tainted wine to her.

"Ready for the tour?" Brett asked.

She stood from the couch.

"Let's start out back," Brett said. He walked to the back of the living room and opened the door leading out to the expansive patio and pool area. After a half-hour walk around the grounds, he brought Monica back to the front of the house. He could tell by her stumbling that the drugs were taking effect. She'd finished her drink fifteen minutes prior. Brett punched in the code for the garage. The first door of three opened. His Jeep sat in that garage stall.

"Come on," Brett said. "We'll go through here so you can see the lower level of the house."

Monica walked to him and put her arms around his neck. She pressed a leg between his. "Why don't you show me your bedroom," she said.

"Are you telling me you can't wait until later?" Brett laughed. "Patience. Plus, Harry, the driver, should be here soon."

"I thought you said his name was Henry."

The drugs weren't working quickly enough on the woman—she was still coherent enough to catch his error. Brett improvised. "It is. Sometimes, I call him by his last name. It's spelled *H-a-r-i.*"

She slowly nodded, seeming to buy his explanation. "Maybe we can just stay here. I'm sure we can find something to do that will be fun," Monica said.

Brett looked her in the eyes as she smiled at him. Her eyes were beginning to glaze over as though she was extremely intoxicated.

"Yeah, if you want. Let's grab another glass of wine."

He ushered Monica inside and parked her on the couch again. He went to the kitchen and fixed her another Rohypnol-filled glass of wine. When he brought the glass to her, she was passed out with her chin resting on her chest.

"It's about time," Brett said.

Monica woke up. "It's what? Time? For what?"

"Here." He handed her the glass of wine and took a seat next to her.

She brought it to her mouth and took a sip. "Where's yours?" she asked.

"I was about to go to the kitchen to get it."

Monica set the glass of wine down on the glass coffee table. She turned toward Brett and tried to pull him on top of her.

Brett held back.

"Come on. Let's screw around," she said. Her words came slow and slurred.

"Let me call the driver quick and cancel," he said. He pulled his cell phone from his pocket.

Monica picked up her glass and took a large mouthful of wine. She swallowed then clanked the glass back down on the table, spilling some on the rug covering the tile.

Brett pretended to be having a conversation with someone while watching Monica from the corner of his eye. She leaned back on the sofa and closed her eyes as he continued talking to no one on the phone. Then Monica's head fell to her chest—she was out. He planned to give the drugs a few more minutes to work before taking her downstairs.

CHAPTER THIRTEEN

I woke up a bit after seven in the morning, showered, and dressed. I sat at the small desk in my room, putting together a file of everything I wanted to go over with the families during interviews that day. I flipped the folder closed and dialed Karen, who picked up right away.

"Hey," she said.

"Mrs. Rawlings," I said.

"How was your night?" she asked.

I leaned back in my chair. "After I talked to you, I watched some television, had what I figured to be an eighteen-dollar gin and tonic from the minibar, and knocked out. About it. You?"

"I unboxed a few things and curled up with Porkchop on the couch. We watched a couple of sappy movies and cried. Ate popcorn."

I smiled. "Date night with the dog?" I asked.

"Exactly. I'd rather it be you, but I'll take what I can get."

"Thanks, I guess?"

"What time did you say you had to go and meet with

the victim's families today?" Karen asked.

"The first one is at ten," I said. "It sounds like we'll probably have to leave here a bit after nine. Second one is at three this afternoon. Then we have to go this evening and view the scenes where the women were found." A horn honked on her end of the call. "Are you heading into the office now?" I asked.

"Yeah. Some jerk just cut me off."

"I'll let you pay attention to driving," I said.

"Okay. Call me later."

"I will. Love you."

"Love you, too. Be safe," she said.

"Always. Bye." I hung up.

I stood, hung my shoulder holster over myself, and pulled on my suit jacket. I needed a coffee but had never been a fan of the small hotel-room coffee makers and the kind of coffee they brewed—plus, I'd seen that the hotel had a coffee shop just outside the front awning. I put on my shoes and left my room. After a quick elevator ride down to the lobby, I left the hotel, made a right, and walked next door. The aroma from the coffee shop could be smelled from the sidewalk. I entered, and the inside of the coffee shop was a red-and-white nineteen-fifties theme. I headed to the counter, ordered two cups of what the barista recommended, filled my jacket pocket with sugar and packaged creamers, and headed back.

I rode the elevator back up and went to Beth's room. I gave her door a knock with the toe of my shoe, and the door swung open. Beth stood before me in nothing but a towel. Her hair was wet. The television remote hung from her hand.

"Um," I said. "Guess I should have maybe called first.

I got you a coffee." I held it out toward her.

"Set it on the table. Come in."

"Um," I said again. I took a step into the room and set her coffee down, holding the door open with the heel of my shoe. I fished the sugar and creamers from my pocket and set them next to the cup.

Beth went to the edge of the bed and took a seat, staring at the television.

I scratched at the back of my head. "I'll let you get ready. Just come next door when you are."

"Hank, just come in. Close the door. Did you see this?" She jerked her chin at the television and turned up the volume.

"See what?" I asked.

"They found another body in a Dumpster. It might be our guy."

I walked into the room, and the door closed at my back. I stared at the television. "Is this coverage live?" I asked.

"Yeah."

"What have they said?" I asked.

"Not much. It's a female."

"Is this local?" I asked.

She turned her head and looked at me. "Englewood. It's on the south side of Chicago. It looks like some old grocery store or something."

"Did the news give an address?" I asked.

Beth shook her head.

"Get ready," I said. "I'll call for the car."

"Are we going there? What about our appointment with Jasmine Thomas's mother at ten?" she asked. "We still need to stop at the local office and get those records as well."

I thought for a second. The body in the Dumpster might not have been related, and I wasn't the biggest fan of missing appointments with family members of murder victims. "Do you mind making the stop for the records?" I asked.

"Not at all," Beth said.

"Okay. I'll go check out the scene of this body dump and then meet you at the interview with the mother."

"Sure. That works," she said.

I used Beth's room phone to call downstairs for my car, stopped at my room to grab the interview folder I'd created, and left. After a half dozen phone calls, I got through to Agent Andrews and got the exact location of the scene. When I let him know I was on my way, he said he was just arriving on location. I punched the address into my cell phone's navigation—just ten miles away.

The drive took a half hour due to traffic—traffic I was forced to sit through because I didn't have an official car with lights or a siren.

News vans with masts in the air littered the sides of the street around what was an out-of-business grocery store. The front of the rectangular building read Discount Groceries and Checks Cashed in paint across the windows. Numerous squad cars were keeping the rubberneckers at bay and the scene secure. I slipped my car down the news-van-filled side street and pointed the nose toward the Chicago PD Ford SUV blocking the driveway to the building. An officer walked up, so I lowered my window and removed my credentials from my pocket.

"Agent Rawlings, FBI," I said.

"One second." The officer turned and headed to the

Ford. He backed it up enough that I could pull into the lot.

I drove in and pulled off to one side, next to a pair of what looked like government-issued Crown Victoria sedans.

The officer who had moved the SUV approached.

"The scene is behind the building here," the officer said. "There are a handful of agents already back there."

"Got it. Thank you," I said. I walked the lot to the yellow police tape segmenting off what looked like an alley spanning the back of the grocery store. I pulled my bifold and showed my credentials to the officer at the tape.

The officer waved me through. "All the way in the back of the alley at the Dumpster," he said.

I headed back, passing officers and what looked like a forensics unit looking around. Miscellaneous yellow evidence cones marked the cement. Two blue FBI jackets caught my eye. I walked over. Both men had their backs to me. One of the men appeared to be Agent Andrews, judging by the short blond hair. The other was short and round, a coffee in his right hand. The rounder of the two turned toward me. His hair was short, brown, and balding. He had hound-dog jowls and a line of sweat over his brow. His face looked as if he'd missed the last few mornings of shaving.

Then Andrews turned. "Agent Rawlings, this is Agent Frank Toms. He's from my office."

I shook the other agent's hand. "Good to meet you." Then I addressed Agent Andrews. "Is this our guy?"

"It looks like it. Female DB in a Dumpster. Needle marks consistent with the others."

"Who found her?" I asked.

"Some scrappers called her in," Agent Toms said.

"Scrappers?" I asked.

"Guys driving around looking for junk metal to recycle. They came in the alley; flipped the lid on the Dumpster, looking for junk; and saw the body. Called the local PD. The local PD called us."

"They were questioned?" I asked.

"Yeah. Just a couple of scrappers. Nothing there," Agent Andrews said.

"Is the body still here?" I asked.

Agent Andrews shook his head. "They took her about a half hour ago after the forensics team was done with her."

"Do you want to walk me through the scene here and maybe get whoever is heading up the forensics unit over here? I'd like to talk to him," I said.

"Yeah, I'll walk you through." He looked at Agent Toms. "Frank, why don't you hunt down Nick."

Agent Toms gave him a nod and walked off.

Agent Andrews walked me to the Dumpster. The lid was flipped open. I glanced inside—about a foot of old garbage filled the bottom. I spotted an old computer monitor, some glass beer bottles, and random garbage. I caught a faint whiff of what smelled like bleach over the stink of old garbage.

"Do you smell bleach?" I asked.

"I caught a hint of it before, yeah. Forensics thinks she may have been scrubbed down. I'm not sure there was mention of that in any of the files."

"I know I didn't see it." I pulled out my notepad and made a note of it. "It could just be that the other bodies had been in the Dumpsters longer. The smell could have dissipated."

Andrews bobbed his head, appearing to agree.

"We dusted and photographed everything. Nick, from our forensics team, can show you the photos on his camera. She was in here, facing up. The coroner put the time of death between forty-eight and seventy-two hours," Andrews said.

I looked away from my notepad, at Andrews. "Do we know how much of that time she was in this Dumpster?" I asked.

He shook his head. "Not sure. She obviously wasn't killed in the Dumpster, so less time than that."

"Any ID, phone, or anything on her?"

"No phone but a purse with photo identification. The woman's name was Rebecca Wright. Twenty-six years old." Andrews ran his free hand over his head. "Just a kid."

I wrote down the woman's name and age. "Was she local?" I asked.

"Chicago area, yeah," he said.

I pointed back up the alley. "The evidence cones. What did you guys find?"

"A couple of cigarette butts and a wad of gum. No idea if it belonged to our guy, but we figured we should mark them off and gather them for DNA."

I nodded.

I noticed Agent Toms standing with a man in a white clean suit and yellow rubber gloves—a camera hung from a strap around his neck. "Is that the forensics guy there?" I asked.

"Yeah, Nick Freeman. He's our lead," Agent Andrews said.

"I'm going to go have a talk with him. I'll be back with

you in a minute."

I flipped my notepad closed, put it back into my pocket, and headed over to Agent Toms and the forensics lead.

Toms walked back toward Andrews as I approached.

"Agent Rawlings," I said.

Blond hair stuck out from the edges of the hood on his clean suit. "Nick Freeman," he said.

"Do you have the photos from the scene?" I asked.

"Yeah, one second. Let me get them pulled up." He took the camera in his hands and pulled the strap over his head. He pulled up the photos and faced the camera's screen toward me before advancing through them.

The photos were of the woman contorted in the Dumpster. Large sunglasses covered her eyes. The woman's arms were out to her sides, her legs bent at the knees. Her hair looked to be dyed blond, from the half inch of darker roots, and pulled back in a ponytail. She wore a black shirt and a small pair of denim shorts. One of her shoes was half off of her heel. The next photos were of bruising and needle marks to her arms and thighs. The following photos were more of the same, but to the sides of the woman's neck. It was, without a doubt, the exact method used to kill the previous women. I went through a few more things with the forensics lead and thanked him.

Then I caught the time on my watch—twenty after nine.

I walked back to Agent Andrews, who gave me his attention.

"I have an appointment to interview some family from the other victims in a bit here, so I'll have to head out," I said. "When do you think you'll have everything from the scene here put together and in a file?"

"I'm on until five tonight, but I'm sure I'll be at our HQ later than that, wrapping up. We should have a case file before I leave for the night," Andrews said.

"Okay. Either Agent Harper or myself will be by to pick up a copy if that's all right."

"Absolutely. I'll leave it at the front for you if I'm out of the office by the time you make it over."

"Appreciate that."

He nodded.

CHAPTER FOURTEEN

I called Ball in Manassas and let him know we had another homicide. He was going to pull up everything he could on the woman and get it over to me as soon as possible. I dialed Beth, who picked up within two rings.

"Is it our guy?" she asked.

"Yeah," I said. "I got the victim's information over to Ball back at headquarters. Andrews was on the scene. He's going to have a file ready for us to pick up by the end of the workday. Where are you?" I asked.

"Headed out from the FBI building now. I just picked up all of our records. It's going to take me about a half hour to get to Jasmine Thomas's mother's place. Were you still planning on meeting me there?"

"Yeah. I just got in the car. Send me over the address."

"Sure, you'll see it in a second," Beth said.

"I'll be watching for it."

"Okay. See you in a bit," Beth said then hung up.

The address came from Beth a moment later. I pulled it up on my cell phone's GPS app and hit the button to navigate. The robotic woman's voice told me the drive would be thirty-five minutes. I followed the suggested route to what looked like a middle-class neighborhood. All the homes appeared to have been built in the nineteen seventies. Some still had dark-brown exteriors, some were brick, and others appeared to have been updated to keep with the times. I slowed when I saw Beth's rental car parked along the road. Pulling in behind her car, I glanced at the home up the driveway to my right. Above the garage in black numbers was the address I was looking for. The home itself was a light-brick single story with black faux shutters around the exterior windows. A handful of mature trees stood in the yard—each wrapped with a small flower garden.

I grabbed the interview folder I'd put together and stepped from the car.

The driver's door on Beth's rental opened—I hadn't even noticed she was inside.

"Waiting long?" I asked.

She looked at her watch. "A couple minutes. I figured I'd wait for you. It's just going on ten now, so we're right on time. You can fill me in on everything you got over at the scene when we're through here."

I nodded, and we made our way up the driveway to the front door. A mat under my feet read The Murphys. I looked through the front bay window to my left and saw a couple seated on the couch, staring at a television. I reached out and knocked on the door.

The seated woman looked at me through the window and stood. The door opened a moment later.

"Ma'am," I said. "I'm Agent Rawlings, and this is Agent Harper with the FBI."

The woman wore a light-colored patterned blouse and

a pair of shorts. Her hair was brown and shoulder length. She appeared to be in her fifties. Her eyes were pink and puffy from crying. The woman was holding a tissue and pressed it against her nose. She sniffed and invited us in.

"I'm Cheryl Murphy." She nodded to the seated man, who stood. "My husband, Tony, Jasmine's stepfather."

"Mr. Murphy," I said.

The man wore a pair of blue jeans and a plaid long-sleeved shirt with breast pockets. His hair was finger length and white, and he appeared a few years older than his wife. He pointed at the television. "The body that was found in Englewood. Is it the same guy that…" His voice trailed off.

"It looks to be similar, yes," I said. "We can't say definitively yet. The investigation has just gotten underway."

The couple didn't respond.

Beth asked, "Did you want to talk in here, or…?"

"We can sit in the dining room at the table," Mr. Murphy said.

We followed the wife through the living room and took seats around a rectangular dining table just off to the side of the kitchen. I noticed photos of the woman's daughter standing in a corner bookshelf. The husband grabbed a box of tissues from the living room, set it in front of his wife, and took a seat beside her.

Mrs. Murphy pulled a few tissues from the box and dabbed at her eyes. "We've spoken with the police. We've already spoken with the FBI," she said. "No one is doing anything—it's been a week without as much as an update. And now there's another murdered girl that might be related."

Beth spoke up. "The local Chicago branch of the FBI requested us from Virginia to help with the investigation entailing your daughter. We met with the local branch yesterday and got everything they had on the case. We'd like to go over some of that with you firsthand."

"They requested you from Virginia? What are you? Special special agents?" Mr. Murphy asked.

"You could say that. We work in a division that only handles these matters," Beth said.

"You mean serial killers?" Mr. Murphy asked.

Beth dipped her head in confirmation.

"Anything we can do to help find whoever did this to our daughter," Mrs. Murphy said.

I looked at Beth. "I'll let you go first, then I'll ask what I'd like to ask."

"Sure," Beth said. She looked at the couple. "If you don't mind, I'd like to record our conversation," Beth said.

"For?" Mr. Murphy asked.

"Just so I don't miss anything."

They gave her permission.

Beth thumbed the button to start her voice recorder and began gathering information on the couple's daughter. Jasmine Thomas had been twenty-nine years old and divorced. She lived alone—no children. Her mother informed us that she worked some dead-end job in retail for an office-supply company. Her father had been deceased since Jasmine was eleven. The man listed as her father, whom Beth had called, was actually the man sitting in front of us, Tony Murphy. Jasmine had been single. The last conversation Jasmine had with her mother went like countless conversations before it—Mrs. Murphy said nothing seemed off with her daughter. Beth concluded her questioning and left the interview to me.

"Was your daughter close friends with anyone other than…" I looked for the name on my sheet. "Andrea Fradet. She's the only friend we had listed."

"I'm sure she had friends or acquaintances at work," Mrs. Murphy said. "She mentioned a few people by name there during our normal day-to-day conversations. She never did anything with anyone outside of work, though. She mostly just sat at home, or if she did do something, shopping or whatever, it was with Andrea. Those two have been close since they were little." She brought her tissue up to her nose and wiped. "Sorry, 'had been' close," she added.

Her husband rubbed her shoulder.

I gave her a moment while I jotted down the details of the friendship in my notes.

"Have you spoken to Andrea yet?" Mrs. Murphy asked.

"No. But we plan to," I said.

I flipped open my folder with the driver's-license photos of the other victims. I pulled the pages out and handed them to the couple. "Do any of these women or their names seem familiar to you?"

The couple looked briefly and handed them back.

"No," Mr. Murphy said.

Mrs. Murphy shook her head.

I put the photos back into the folder. "You said your daughter was single. Was she actively dating different men?"

"No. Not really. She saw a handful of different people occasionally. She'd mentioned the name Tom and another named Mark. They seemed to be passing things, so I didn't keep up too much. If there was ever someone serious, she would have brought him over."

I wrote the names of the men down. "Last names for either man?" I asked.

She shook her head.

"These men, how did she meet them?" I asked.

"She was on a dating website, I think. I couldn't tell you which one, though," Mrs. Murphy said.

"Do you think there would be a way we could find out?" I asked.

"We have her bank statements, honey," Mr. Murphy said. "There might be something there."

The wife nodded.

The man stood and walked from the kitchen.

I didn't know if I should tell the guy we already had her bank records sitting in a box in the car. I figured Beth would have said something if she didn't need or want him to go and retrieve them.

"We have all of her belongings from her apartment in the garage," Mrs. Murphy said. "I haven't brought myself to go through them yet."

I didn't know how to respond, so I remained quiet.

Beth reached out and touched the woman's hand. "We're going to do everything we can."

Mr. Murphy walked back in with three sheets of paper in his hand. He took a pair of reading glasses from the breast pocket of his shirt and put them on. Then he leaned against the kitchen counter facing the dining room where we sat as he flipped the pages. He ran his finger down the deposits and withdrawals. "I don't see any dating services listed," he said. Mr. Murphy looked at his wife. "You're sure she never said what site she used?"

Mrs. Murphy shook her head.

The husband handed the sheets to me. I looked them over and glanced at the ending monthly balance of twenty-eight dollars. I thanked him and handed back the bank records.

"Were those current-month records?" Beth asked.

He looked at the sheets of paper and nodded. "Did you want me to make you a copy?" he asked.

"Sure," Beth said.

"Just give me one minute." The husband walked down a hall next to the dining room and turned into another room.

I looked at Mrs. Murphy. "Did she have a computer?" I asked.

"She had a laptop. It's in the garage. I couldn't tell you what the password is to access it, though," Mrs. Murphy said. "Do you think that whoever did this maybe found her online somehow?"

"There's no way for us to tell at the moment, but we'd like to find out," I said. "It may help to get whatever computers the victims, including your daughter, had in the hands of our tech-department guys. You never know—there may be something there that we can connect the dots with."

"Let me see what my husband says," she said.

Mr. Murphy walked back into the dining room and handed me copies of the bank records, which I slipped into my folder. "Says about what?" he asked.

"They'd like Jasmine's computer so their tech guys can go through it. They think there's a chance they may be able to get some information from it."

"Would we expect to get it back?" Mr. Murphy asked.

"If there is nothing on it that leads anywhere, absolutely. If there is, the computer would be used as evidence," Beth said.

Mr. Murphy looked at his wife.

"Let them have it," she said.

The husband went back to the garage and returned a moment later with a black laptop case. "The computer is inside." He set it on the dining-room table.

I went through another half hour's worth of questioning with the parents, just trying to get a better idea of the person their daughter was. Beth and I left their house a few minutes after noon and drove back to the hotel.

CHAPTER FIFTEEN

Monica's body lay upon his embalming table. Brett had just slipped the needles into her thighs. A soothing calm came over him as he watched the blood flow. He knelt and watched it as it worked its way through the plastic tubing. The blood reached the end and ran out, into the drain in the floor. Brett took the tube in hand and let the blood flowing from the end cascade over his fingers.

He looked up. From his kneeling position, he could just see Monica's left hand hanging off the side of the table. "I have to say, Monica, I guess I've always had a thing with blood. I don't know when it really started—probably six or seven. I had to go live in a boys' home for a bit. The place was a real dump. Rats would climb through the walls at night. I started catching them and killing them. I guess I was just bored. I found it enjoyable to watch them bleed. Then I got shipped off to live with some foster parents. They didn't care for me all that much. All they cared about was getting the checks from the state. They never really noticed I was there until I twisted the head off of a pigeon that flew into the front window of the house. I squeezed the blood from its body all over the living-room carpet. The foster parents found me with it in the living room. I blamed it on the cat, said it must have dragged it in from outside. The cat's name was Sprinkles. He was a gray tabby. I killed him the next day."

He stood and poked his blood-covered fingers into the center of her forehead.

"Those foster parents shipped me back to the boys' home. The people in charge there thought it would be right to have me see a shrink. I did and spent years in therapy. Care to guess the first human I killed?"

Monica, unconscious, didn't respond.

"Nope. Not the shrink. I killed Sally Best when I was twelve. She was the same age. Another foster family picked me up and welcomed me into their home. I went to school, got okay grades. Sally was popular but seemed nice, though she'd never talked to me. Well, I mustered up the courage to ask her to the fall dance. I figured all the other kids were going and it would be the normal thing to do. I made her a little card with a heart drawn on it. I asked her to circle yes or no to the question if she'd go with me. She ripped up the card I made right in front of me.

She looked me in the eyes, laughed, and called me a creepy little weirdo. I can still hear her voice. The rest of the class joined in her laughter. Little Sally never made it home from school that day. Something happened to her on her walk: she accidently tripped and fell in front of a car."

Brett went to Monica's right arm and inserted a needle into a vein at her elbow.

"Do you want to know how many people I've killed?"

Brett looked at her face.

The woman lay motionless.

Brett smiled. "That wall there behind your head is one of three. That's not even close to all of them. The older I get, the more I perfect everything. I used to be reckless, killing every few months. Now I just do it in spurts—usually about five or ten at a time and then take years off. Give everyone enough time to forget about it, you know? I started with that after the wife and I got divorced. I was so happy with my newfound freedom that I went on a little rampage, turns out a bunch at once was just what the doctor ordered. Anyway, as I matured, I developed methods, systems, if you will. Hell, my business was created to allow me to do this. It surprised the shit out of me that it made me rich. Which only helps my system work better, by the way. Yup. I travel all over. I vary my methods every now and again but usually come back to the needles and tubes—it's clean."

Brett took the two remaining needles and tubes from the washbasin and slipped them into the carotid arteries on each side of her neck.

Monica's body remained motionless.

Brett stood over her and watched. He followed the blood running from the tubes with his eyes for minutes. He dipped his head and placed his ear next to her nose and mouth. Her breathing was rapid. He swiped his hand down her arm—it was cool and clammy to the touch.

"Not long now," he said. "What you're experiencing is called hypovolemic shock. Do you know what that is?"

Monica, again, didn't respond.

"I didn't know what it was called at first either—I had to look it up when I started doing it this way years ago.

Basically, it's your body shutting down when the blood drains from it. I'd say you're at about forty-percent blood loss right now." He shook his head and bit his lip. "No coming back after a forty-percent blood loss."

CHAPTER SIXTEEN

I took a seat at the desk in my room and set down the file box Beth had picked up from the local FBI office. Beth followed me in, and the door closed at her back. I caught the time. We had an hour and fifteen minutes before we had to leave for our next family interview.

"Why didn't you tell the husband we already had the bank records?" I asked.

She shrugged. "They were offering. When someone offers up something, just take it. It allows the family to feel like they are helping."

"Makes sense," I said.

"Lunch, while you let me know what you got out in Englewood?" Beth asked.

I let out a breath. "I guess I probably have to eat since I missed breakfast."

"Do you want to just hit the same place we did yesterday?" Beth asked. "It looks like we only have an hour or so."

"Yeah, that's fine. The food and prices were decent," I said.

"Ready now?" she asked.

"Yeah." I nodded toward the door and followed Beth out.

We walked the hall, and she thumbed the button for the elevator. The doors opened and we stepped inside.

"When I called back Hilary Wormack, the mother of Angela, and asked about Angela's computer, she said she had it and will turn it over to us when we meet with her," I said. "If we can get one from Kennedy Taylor's family, it looks like we'll have three for the tech guys to look into."

"Perfect," Beth said.

"Is that something that we send back to Manassas or have the local branch check out?"

"Local," Beth said. "You said Agent Andrews was going to have a case file for us on the most recent by the end of the day?"

"Yeah."

"We'll drop the computer or computers off then if we get one from Kennedy Taylor's family."

I nodded.

The elevator doors let us out into the lobby. We headed down the two flights of blue-carpeted stairs and outside. After leaving the hotel, we walked around the block to the restaurant. The hostess sat us in the exact same booth as the day prior. Beth and I quickly browsed the menus and put in our order. I ordered the same thing as the last time—the Philly cheesesteak sandwich had been pretty good.

"What did Ball say when you called him and told him we had another?" Beth asked.

"He said, 'Your killer is there, and you two are there. Find him.'"

"That sounds about right. What was the scene like?"

"News vans and local PD everywhere. Agent Andrews had another guy and the FBI's forensics team there with him. The body was gone, but I saw the photos that were taken of her while she was still inside the Dumpster."

"And?" Beth asked.

"Woman in a Dumpster. Faint smell of bleach. Not much of any evidence. Close-up photos showed needle marks and bruising in the same locations. Ball is sending me everything he could get on the woman. Um, hold on." I pulled out my cell phone and looked at the screen because I had a message from Supervisor Ball, probably my information on the deceased woman. I opened the e-mail. "Rebecca Wright. Twenty-six years old. Hair is listed as brown on her DL though it was dyed blond in person. Address is in Elgin. Single. Here, I'll forward this over to you." I clicked the prompts to send her the woman's information.

Beth pulled out her phone. "Got it." She opened the message and read over the woman's information. "Do you think there is anything to how they look?" she asked. "Or maybe what all these women have in common?"

"Well, they're all single. All thin. They're all fairly attractive, I guess." I thought about it further. "All in a small age range of between twenty-five and thirty. None of these women had kids, did they?"

Beth shook her head. "So our killer definitely has a type of woman that he's after."

"Appears so," I said. "But since when? It looked like the past victims, from years back, were all over the place. I mean, they were all women, but the ages spanned into the forties, and it didn't seem like body type mattered."

"Yeah, that is true," Beth said.

Our waitress passed, dropping off our drinks.

Beth held her straw like a knife and tapped it against the table to pull off the wrapper. Then she plunged it into her iced tea and took a sip. "So we have a type of woman that he's after now. Besides that, what have we learned new since we've been here?"

"Not a ton," I said.

"Well, we have their bank and phone records back at the hotel. We have a pretty good idea that our killer is dating these women in some form or another. I'd think if they all were on the same dating website, it would have been found by the local FBI when they went through the records. Maybe we have one man finding women from multiple websites," Beth said.

"Plausible," I said. "But I still think that it would have been found. Four dead women all on dating websites, whether the same or not, should raise a flag."

Beth rocked her head back and forth. "Yeah, I guess that would be too big to miss. I still think our guy is a suitor somehow. It just makes the most sense. Usually, when something makes the most sense, it's right."

"I can't argue with you there."

Our food came a moment later, and we ate quickly and headed back to the hotel. Beth had her car brought up by the valet, and we left for our interview with Kennedy Taylor's family.

I sat in the passenger seat, going through her information. Ms. Taylor was listed as living in Oak Brook, Illinois. "Parents said they were having some kind of a gathering there today?" I asked.

"Yeah."

"We're not walking into a memorial or after-funeral thing for this girl, are we?" I asked.

"I don't know. I spoke with her father. He gave us a time to come and just said that there would be people close to her there that we could speak with."

I nodded but said nothing.

Beth exited the freeway and drove us into in affluent-appearing neighborhood. Each house appeared twenty or so years old, yet none of them looked remotely affordable. The cars in the driveways were all high-end, shiny and new.

"Guessing the Taylor family has money," I said.

"If they live back here or, hell, anywhere in this town, they do. These are about the smallest houses around here, though. Still probably a million each," she said. "Their house is going to be down the next street on our right."

Beth made a right up the block. Two blocks down, I saw a line of cars along the curb. Beth slowed and parked behind the last car. "The address should be a couple of houses up on our right here."

We stepped out of the car. I tucked the file under my arm, and we headed for the Taylor's house. The home came into view behind a couple of large oak trees. The U-shaped driveway was full of cars. Set back from the street was a light-colored brick single-story home with an unusually steeply pitched cedar-shake roof. We walked up the driveway toward the house. I didn't see a garage, but a part of the driveway stretched forward down the far side of the house. The home had six windows on the front, divided by a door in the center. To the left and right of the arched front door were a pair of rectangular windows in arched alcoves. The windows on each end of the house were square, with light-blue shutters matching the color of the front door. I thought the color of the door and shutters was an odd choice, though I couldn't say it looked entirely bad.

Beth and I stepped up to the landing of the front door.

"Do you have a name of the girl's father you spoke with?" I asked.

"Doug." Beth reached out and thumbed the doorbell, and we waited.

A moment later, the front door pulled open, and a man stood before us. He appeared in his early fifties. He was roughly my size and weight—a few inches over six foot and around two hundred pounds. He had a strong dimpled chin and short dark hair with a bit of gray sprinkled in. The man wore a yellow polo shirt with khaki shorts.

"We're here to see Doug Taylor," Beth said.

"I'm Doug. Are you the agent I spoke with on the phone?" he asked.

Beth nodded.

"Why don't you two come in, and we'll head up to my office," he said.

With that comment, the shape of the roofline made a little more sense—the home must have had a second story that faced the backyard of the property. We followed him inside. He led us through the foyer and toward the kitchen in the back of the house. Four women, seated and talking, surrounded a gray granite island in the center of the kitchen. Through the windows of the back of the house, I spotted about twenty people in the home's back patio area. Mr. Taylor turned left from the kitchen and opened a door. He walked through and up a flight of stairs as Beth and I followed.

The upstairs was a single large office. A big wooden desk sat at the back of the room. One window overlooked the backyard. Miscellaneous awards covered the wall area behind his desk. A television took up the wall opposite the window, and a few lounge chairs and a small couch stood before it.

"You guys can have a seat here." He gestured toward the couch.

Beth and I sat.

Mr. Taylor turned one of the lounge chairs toward the couch and took a seat. He clasped his hands in his lap. "We're having a service for Kennedy at our church tonight." He ran the knuckle of one index finger back and forth under his nose. "Friends and family from the area is who you saw downstairs and outside. Has there been any news?"

"We're still investigating. Trying to gather everything we can," Beth said. "It's the reason for our visit."

"Okay," he said. "Whatever you need."

Though the guy was keeping up a good composure, I could see pain in his eyes—they had an almost hollow look, as if nothing behind them.

"We'd just like to know more about your daughter's personal life. Little things that may not seem important but could maybe help us to connect her with some of the other victims. If we can connect them, it could lead us straight to the person responsible," I said.

"Okay. Give me a minute. I'd like to go get my wife and daughter and have them come up."

"Sure," I said.

CHAPTER SEVENTEEN

Doug Taylor reentered the office with two women in tow. "This is my wife Tanya and our daughter Cassidy," he said.

Beth and I stood and shook the hands of the two women. The mother, Tanya Taylor, looked to be in her late forties or early fifties. She had blond shoulder-length hair and wore a white blouse and shorts with some kind of charm necklace around her neck. Her skin was dark—too dark for a natural tan.

The daughter, Cassidy Taylor, looked to be in her midtwenties. She had a thin face, big eyes, long dark hair, and glasses that she seemed to be hiding behind. She wore a small orange T-shirt and white shorts. Her tan was also dark yet not as extreme as her mother's. The mother and daughter took seats in the lounge chairs beside the couch while Doug Taylor rolled his office chair from behind his desk and brought it to his wife's side and took a seat.

"We we're telling Mr. Taylor here that we would just like to get some more information on Kennedy's personal life," I said.

"However we can help," Mrs. Taylor said.

The daughter, Cassidy, said nothing.

"If you don't mind, I'd like to record our conversation," Beth said.

"That's fine," Mr. Taylor said.

Beth removed her voice recorder from her pocket and thumbed the button. A little red light illuminated on its side.

"Special Agents Harper and Rawlings sitting with Doug Taylor, Tanya Taylor, and Cassidy Taylor, the family of Kennedy Taylor." Beth turned her attention to the family. "We would like to start by asking about the last time you saw Kennedy."

Mrs. Taylor sniffed and wiped her nose. "Two days before she was found."

"Um," Beth said. "We had it as the prior day in our file."

"She went to work on Thursday. Left here about ten in the morning for a lunch shift. Normally, she would be home by around five thirty, but sometimes she'll work a bell-to-bell, which would mean that she wouldn't get home until after midnight, when we'd normally be asleep. We woke up Friday morning, and she wasn't here. We tried calling her but never got an answer."

I looked through my file and didn't notice anything that mentioned where she'd been employed. "Where is it that Kennedy worked?" I asked.

"The place is called The Pub. It's a trendy restaurant slash sports bar about twenty minutes from here."

I jotted it down. "Now, when you called her, did the phone go straight to voice mail?" I asked.

Mrs. Taylor nodded.

"Do you have her phone?" I asked.

"It was never found," Mr. Taylor said.

I made a note of that. "Did you speak with anyone at her employer to see what time she was actually there until?"

"We did. We spoke with a couple people. She left around five o'clock, alone," Mr. Taylor said.

Mrs. Taylor wiped her eyes with the back of her hand. "They found her Sunday morning out in Elk Grove Village."

"And her vehicle?" I asked. "We have it here that it was never located."

"Still hasn't been found," Mr. Taylor said.

I nodded.

"What was Kennedy's relationship status? Was she single?" Beth asked.

"She was. She lived with a boyfriend for a couple years. They split up about six months ago, and she moved back in here. She wanted to just rent her own place, but we were kind of pushing her to stay here for a bit, save a little money, and try to purchase a home," Mr. Taylor said.

"Was she dating anyone?" I asked.

"No," Mrs. Taylor said.

"Yeah, she was," Cassidy said.

Mrs. Taylor looked at her daughter. "I didn't know that. Who?"

"I don't know. Some guy. She said he was older."

"Do you have a name?" I asked.

"Rick."

"Last name?" I asked.

She shook her head.

In my notepad, I jotted down the first name and the

fact that Kennedy Taylor had been dating.

"How have I never heard of this?" Mrs. Taylor asked.

"I don't know," Cassidy said. "The guy was older. She thought you guys wouldn't approve. The guy had money, though. Kennedy said he had a black Ferrari."

I wrote the piece of information in my notepad.

"I actually think she was only seeing the guy because of his money."

"Do you know how she met this guy?" Beth asked.

"I think he had an ad up on the singles section of Classified OD."

I wrote that down. I knew the website. Everyone knew the website. What the OD stood for, I didn't know—it could have been "overdrive," "overdose," or "on demand"—I'd heard it referred to as each. What I did know was that it was one of the larger classified websites in the US. You could buy, sell, trade, offer services, hire people for jobs, and meet people with their singles section. Everything on the website was completely free to use. If she'd met the guy there, we wouldn't find any bank records to verify it, which got me thinking that all of our victims could have met the guy there and we wouldn't have known it. However, a browsing history of websites on their computers might show us.

"How certain are you on the fact that she met this guy on that specific site?" I asked.

"I'm pretty sure that was the site," Cassidy said.

"Sure enough to give us a sworn statement that she did?" I asked.

She shrugged and slowly shook her head. "Um, I don't think so. I know she used the site, and I'm pretty sure, but not one-hundred-percent, without a doubt, sure."

"Okay. Did she ever show you a photo of this man?" I asked.

"No," she said.

"Did she use her phone or a computer to access the website?" Beth asked.

"Her phone and tablet. She had a regular desktop computer, but she never had it set up since she moved back in here."

I looked at Mr. Taylor. "Do you have access to this tablet she owned?"

"It's in her room. Hold on, I'll go and get it." Mr. Taylor rose from his desk chair and left the room.

"She has a password on it," Cassidy said. "Well, not a password but one of those things where you swipe your finger around a group of dots and it has to be done in a certain arrangement to unlock it."

"Do you know the arrangement?" Beth asked.

Cassidy shook her head.

I looked at Mrs. Taylor, who also shook her head.

Beth reached into her pocket, slipped out her cell phone, and looked at the screen. "I'm actually going to have to take this. Excuse me." She left the voice recorder with me and left the room.

A moment later, Mr. Taylor returned with his daughter's tablet and what looked like its power charger. "Do you have a way to get past the passkey thing?" he asked.

"The FBI's tech department can. If you don't mind, we'd like to go through it and see if there is anything that could potentially help us catch whoever did this."

He didn't respond.

"I know there may be personal things and information

contained inside. Just know that the bureau will handle it with respect for your daughter."

He pursed his lips and slowly nodded. "Would we be getting it back?" he asked.

"As long as it's not needed for evidence, yes," I said.

He held it out toward me. "I think the battery is dead. It doesn't power on. Take the charger with it."

"Thanks," I said.

"I can get something for you to put it in," Mrs. Taylor said.

She stood, walked behind the office desk, and came back with a large padded envelope then placed the tablet inside. I continued asking questions with the family for another ten minutes, and Beth hadn't returned. I was out of things I needed to know and was keeping the family from their guests. I turned off Beth's voice recorder and put it in my pocket. Then I thanked the Taylors for seeing us and let them know I would be in touch. Mr. Taylor walked me from the house, where I saw Beth standing outside near the street, still on the phone. I walked over just as she was hanging up.

"Sorry. Are we done in there?" she asked.

"I went through a few more things with them. It's on the recorder. Figured I'd let them get back to their guests. If we need anything else from them, we can call."

"Is that the tablet?" Beth asked.

I held up the envelope. "Yup."

"Okay."

She started toward the car, and I followed.

"That was Andrea Fradet, Jasmine Thomas's friend, on the phone," Beth said.

"And?"

"Jasmine met a guy in the personals section of the same classifieds website Cassidy just mentioned. This girl, Andrea, will give us a statement to the fact. The soonest she can meet with us is tomorrow. I guess she's out of town. I set us up for ten in the morning. She lives out in Shaumburg."

"Okay. She's one-hundred-percent sure?" I asked. "Give a name of the guy?"

"She didn't know his name but swears to the site. We need to get the computer in the trunk—and that tablet— over to the local bureau's tech guys."

"It's our next stop either way," I said. "Hopefully, they can do something with them while we're there. We don't have to be out to the sixteenth district to view the dump sites until eight, right?"

"Yeah. Figure an hour of driving between going to the Chicago bureau and getting out to the sixteenth district. It will leave the tech guys a couple hours to come up with something. That's if they can get on it right away."

We got in the car, and Beth started it up and pulled a U-turn.

"What is our turnaround time on getting warrants and subpoenas?" I asked.

"Pretty quick, provided Jim is in the office. Why?" Beth asked.

"We need the information from Classified OD. I know how the place works—they make you create a profile. They have a messaging system. I want to see who Jasmine and Kennedy were talking to."

"Absolutely. We'll need to subpoena the records from their corporate office, I'm guessing."

I pulled my phone from my pocket and logged on to

the classified site. I navigated through the links but found nothing on the site as far as a corporate-office location or phone number—only generic e-mail contact forms were available. The website had a link dedicated to law enforcement, but I didn't put much stock in getting anything in a response that wasn't some generic form letter.

"They don't make it easy to get in touch with them," I said.

"Call Ball. He'll have the twins find who to contact. Jim will be able to get us the required paperwork," Beth said. "But I'm betting we need a sworn statement first."

"Let me call and see." I dialed Agent Ball, who answered within a few rings.

"Ball," he said.

"It's Rawlings. We have something that needs to be looked into."

"Sure. What have you got?" he asked.

"Communications from our victims through the Classified OD website. We have two victims that may have met men through the website's personals section. I'd like to get the transcripts of who they were communicating with as well as see if the other victims were using the site. I'm guessing we'll have to subpoena them for the information."

"Okay. Well, a big company like that is going to lawyer the crap out of us, so we'll damn well have to know for certain that the victims were on that site. Do we have any kind of hard evidence that they did in fact use it?"

"We have a friend of Jasmine Thomas who will give us a sworn statement. We can't get it until tomorrow, though. We have a sister of Kennedy Taylor that also says

Kennedy used the site but can't swear to it."

"Do we know that they were planning on meeting with these men prior to going missing?"

"No," I said, "but that's where the transcripts would obviously help. We do have confirmation that all the victims were dating. We have a computer and a tablet from two victims, which we are taking to the local branch of the bureau now to see if we can get something from them."

"Okay. Let me make a few calls and see if I can get anything as far as friendly cooperation. If I can't get anywhere with that, we'll at least need a sworn statement before we can get the required documents to force their hand. I'll call you back shortly."

"Thanks," I said.

Ball hung up.

I looked at Beth. "He says he is going to make a few calls and see if he can get a little friendly cooperation."

She nodded.

CHAPTER EIGHTEEN

Brett pulled the final needle and tube from Monica—she'd been dead since the morning, before he left for work. He took a few steps back from the side of the embalming table to observe his trophy wall, a grid of papers. All were copies of newspaper classified pages, ads on cards left in truck stops, want-to-sell listings from grocery stores, and the like. The most recent were personals listings. Each paper had a photograph of the victim attached.

In the beginning, he used to visit his victims, posing as a buyer for whatever they were selling. He would stop at place after place, looking for the perfect scenario—a woman, alone, not near others. The hunt had been enjoyable, yet it simply took too much time and presented too much risk—a nosy neighbor, a family member showing up, an unexpected guest—countless things that could get him caught. Brett had decided he needed to be able to control the environment.

He ran his finger through the air to the first ad he'd posted on his own website. It was a photo of a different man seeking a woman. Brett had posed as the man and met the woman for lunch. She was pleasantly surprised that he was, in fact, more attractive than his posting. He waited two weeks before asking her over for dinner.

She had come to the house, eaten, and been choked to death before dessert.

A noise from upstairs broke Brett's reminiscing. His cell phone was vibrating and chirping. Brett grumbled and went to the sink. He washed his hands, dried them and headed upstairs.

His phone lay on the coffee table in the living room. Brett walked over and scooped it up. The screen of the phone showed a text message from Carrie, his secretary. The message simply read: *Call the office.*

Brett dialed as he walked down the hall.

"Classified OD. This is Mr. Bailor's office. How can I help you?"

"Hi, Carrie. It's Brett. I just saw your message. What's up?" Brett took a seat at the desk in his home office.

"Well, I was just shutting down for the evening, and I got a call from an FBI agent."

"FBI agent?" Brett asked. "What did he want?"

"He was trying to get a hold of you. He just said that he had an important inquiry and was looking for a call back."

"The nature of the inquiry?" Brett asked.

"He didn't give that information. He just wanted me to pass along the message to you. Did you want me to hand it off to legal, public relations, another executive?"

"Um." Brett thought for a moment. "The agent gave you a callback number, right?"

"Yes. I have it here."

"Let me get that," Brett said. He slid open his desk

drawer and grabbed a pen and a pad of paper from inside.

Carrie gave him the number.

"What was his name?" Brett asked.

"Supervisory Agent Art Ball."

Brett wrote the name down. "And he didn't state the nature of his call at all?"

"No."

"Okay. I'll take care of it. Thanks for the call, Carrie."

"Sure. Did you have your schedule of appointments for tomorrow, or did you need it?"

"I think I have everything. Thanks."

"Have a good night, sir."

"You too."

She hung up.

Brett leaned back in his chair, contemplating why an FBI agent would be trying to contact him directly and how they got the number for his office and how they knew who to call. He woke his computer and punched in the FBI agent's name—he found nothing. Then he dialed the company's legal department. The secretary answered and put him through to Tom Mears, the company's lead attorney.

"Tom Mears," he answered.

"It's Brett Bailor. I just got a message regarding an FBI inquiry."

"FBI inquiry?" Tom asked. "How did that get to you?"

"No idea," Brett said.

"What was the inquiry about?" Tom asked.

"The agent didn't say. My secretary took the call. I've been out of the office since after lunch."

"Did you get a name and number of the person inquiring?"

"I did."

"Why don't you give that to me, and I'll make a call to see what he wants."

Brett gave it to him.

"I'll give you a call back after I see what this is about."

"Thanks, Tom."

"No problem. You'll hear back from me shortly."

Brett hung up.

An uneasy feeling brewed in his gut. His website had dedicated links for law enforcement—they could include the nature of the inquiry, and someone from legal would contact them to provide the required information. For his office to get the call, someone had to specifically search him out. They would have needed to bypass public relations, the company's legal department, the board, and everyone else to get to him. Brett tried searching the agent again, weeding through pages of Internet search results— again, he found nothing. He left the office and went to the kitchen to pour himself a drink. His cell phone rang— Tom was calling back.

"Yeah, Tom."

"I talked to the guy. It was a pretty quick conversation."

"Okay. What did he want?" Brett headed back to his office, whiskey in hand, and took a seat at his desk.

"They are running some kind of an investigation. Basically, they are looking to see if a couple of people were users, and if they were, they'd like the transcripts of their activity and messages—pretty standard law-enforcement inquiry. I basically told them that we couldn't share that information without being subpoenaed specifically for each one. I gave him the information that we would need to be able to provide them with what they sought. How that kind of call got to you, I have no idea."

"Okay, sure. Did he give you the user names or anything?" Brett asked.

"Nah. We've gotten plenty of local law-enforcement requests like this. They'll send a message or call with an inquiry, looking to see if we'll give them what they are asking for voluntarily. Usually when this happens, it means that they don't have enough evidence to get the subpoenas required. The FBI can be a little bit of a different story. They seem to come by the required paperwork a little more easily. I bet the guy gets in contact with us with everything needed."

"So I don't need to call this guy back?"

"I wouldn't think so," Tom said.

"Okay. Appreciate you taking care of it, Tom. We'll talk soon."

"Sure. Have a good night." Tom hung up.

Brett set his phone down, immediately logged into the master system for the website, and searched for each woman he'd had contact with. He needed to be sure that any trace of the women's conversations with him were gone. After twenty minutes of searching, he couldn't find anything between himself and any of them—they had all been successfully deleted from the website's system.

Brett went through a mental checklist. Their phones weren't a problem. The browsing history on their computers wouldn't be a problem. The only thing that could put him and the women together was the standard coffee-shop meetup a day or two prior to him inviting the women over—or out—on a date. Yet all the coffee shops were the mom-and-pop variety and were in different parts of the city. He'd been using a fake name with each woman in case a mention of him came up in one of the women's conversations with friends or family. The photos he used were of someone else—except the one with the Ferrari, but the car was rented and his face wasn't visible.

Brett continued checking things off his mental list.

No place he'd ever dumped a body had any cameras, and the areas he selected were all cross-referenced against the database of Chicago traffic cameras. Each time, he took a different vehicle, sometimes using one from a past victim. He had numerous stolen license plates that he would cycle through. Brett couldn't think of anything that could get him caught. He'd been far too careful.

Brett cracked his knuckles and rocked back in his chair—his heart still thumped rapidly inside his chest. Rehashing in his head every last step he'd taken to be careful still wasn't easing his mind.

I need to know what they want. Are they inquiring about the women?

He stared at the agent's name and number before him on his desk.

What did they call me for?

Brett grabbed his phone and dialed, hoping the fed would give him something.

"Agent Art Ball," a man answered.

"Yes. Hello, this is Brett Bailor. You'd called my office earlier and spoken with my secretary. She was going to have someone from our legal team call you. I just wanted to see if you had been contacted."

"I just got off of the phone with someone a few minutes ago," the agent said.

"Sure. Okay, well I just wanted to follow up personally

since you'd called my office. Did our representative from the legal department answer everything you needed?"

"Well, he didn't really answer anything. Gave me some lawyer talk about getting the subpoenas for the information that we want."

"Um, I guess I never really got the specifics of what the FBI was requesting, so I can't really speak on that." Brett waited a moment before speaking to see if the agent would elaborate.

The agent gave him nothing.

"Was this regarding some form of crime?" Brett asked.

"Yes. We believe that there may have been communications through your website involving multiple victims and a single perpetrator."

"Oh, um, okay." Brett paused, waiting for the agent to expand further.

Again, he didn't.

"So I'm guessing you were looking for records of these individuals and transcripts of communications?" Brett asked.

"Correct."

"Okay. Yeah, for something like that, we would have to have the legal paperwork to get the information to you. We take pride in the privacy of all users. Though, if a crime has been committed, we will do everything we can to furnish the authorities with the documentation requested."

"As long as they have a subpoena," the agent said.

"Yes, we do need the required legal documentation to release user records and interactions."

"Okay, I'll get what we need together and be in touch with your legal department," the agent said.

"Sure. Anything else?"

"That's it. I appreciate the call back," the agent said. The fed gave him nothing further.

"Okay, have a good day." Brett hung up.

Brett let out a hard breath. He'd have to see what the feds were after if or when they produced a subpoena.

CHAPTER NINETEEN

Beth and I had just dropped off Jasmine Thomas's laptop computer and Kennedy Taylor's tablet with the Chicago branch's tech department. They wouldn't be able to get to them until later in the evening or, worst case, the morning. We met shortly with Agent Andrews and grabbed the file on Rebecca Wright, the latest victim. He said he still hadn't spoken with her family but would call us as soon as he made contact. We left the FBI building around six thirty. Beth drove us toward Chicago Police District Sixteen. My phone rang in my pocket—I pulled it out and hit Talk. The call was coming from Agent Ball.

"Rawlings," I said.

"It's Ball calling back."

"Anything?" I asked.

"I had Marcus in the tech unit get me the name and number for the founder of Classified OD. The guy also happens to be listed in the company database as the chief website developer. I figured if we had any chance of getting a little friendly cooperation, it would come from him. I left a message with his secretary and was contacted shortly after by their legal department, letting me know what would be required as far as subpoenas, et cetera to get the information released to us. Basically, they'll want a subpoena per user. I was about to call you back when I got another call from the founder himself, asking if the legal department answered my questions."

"So we got nothing from them is what you're saying?"

"Exactly. We need that sworn statement before we can get the subpoena, and that will just be for her transcripts. Any news on getting anything from the computer or tablet?"

"The tech guys here won't be able to get to them until a little bit later. Beth and I are heading toward the airport area now. We'll probably grab something to eat quickly and then meet with the local PD. They are going to take us to view the dump sites of Jasmine Thomas and Kennedy Taylor."

"The two that were in the same precinct?" Ball asked.

"Correct. Not sure how much good it will do, but it's something."

"Are those tech guys calling you if they get anything from the computer and that tablet?"

"They said they would, yeah."

"Okay. If you guys get anywhere with anything tonight, give me a call. Otherwise, we'll touch base in the morning."

"Sounds good," I said.

Ball hung up.

"News?" Beth asked.

"Not really. Ball left a message with someone there and got a return phone call from a lawyer telling him to get a subpoena per girl, basically."

She nodded.

We neared the airport area around seven o'clock. We stopped for a bite to eat at a fast-food chain and made our way to the Sixteenth Precinct building. Beth pulled past a handful of marked and unmarked cruisers parked in front of the two-story tan brick building—she pulled to the curb and parked. Beth shut the car off, and we stepped out.

"Do we have someone we're supposed to be meeting?" I asked.

"The patrol sergeant I spoke with told me to ask for an Officer Ricodati."

I took the building in as we walked up to the front doors. The two-story glass center section had multicolored windows to break up the space. Beth reached out and pulled the front door open. We walked through the small lobby, passed a pair of benches on each side, and approached a window in the wall separating the actual police department from the lobby.

A man lifted his chin to acknowledge us and spoke from behind a pane of safety glass. "What can I do for you tonight?"

"Agents Beth Harper and Hank Rawlings to see an Officer Ricodati," Beth held her credentials up to the glass.

"Sure, I'll get him paged for you. Should just be a moment."

We left the glass and found one of the benches we'd passed walking in. A minute later, we heard a buzz from the door beside the counter opening.

A patrol officer appearing in his early forties exited the door. He was heavyset, bald, clean shaven, and uniformed. "You're my two agents looking to view the dump sites?"

Beth and I stood.

"We are," Beth said.

We went through a round of introductions with the patrol officer.

"Were you on the scenes?" I asked.

He nodded. "Both."

"Did anything stand out at you?" I asked. "Maybe talk around the station of anything that someone noticed or thought was odd?"

He turned the corner of his mouth to the side and slowly shook his head. "Both were free of anything that could tell us who did it. Both Dumpsters were empty when we found the women. No cameras in the areas—just two women in two different Dumpsters."

"Okay," I said.

"I'm going to grab my cruiser from the lot and meet you out front." He headed for the front door.

Beth and I followed him outside.

"Where are you parked?" he asked.

Beth nodded toward our rental. "That's us there."

"Great. I'll pull up, and you can follow me over to the first. The second site is only a few miles further. It shouldn't take us too long to get over there. A couple minutes," he said.

"Sure," I said.

He made a left for the station's parking lot, and Beth and I got in our car. A minute later, Ricodati pulled alongside our car in his cruiser and waved at us to follow. Beth pulled from the curb, digging in her pocket for her phone. She glanced at the screen.

"It's the local office calling," Beth said, swiping the screen on her phone to answer. "Agent Harper."

I heard the faint sound of someone on the other end of the phone.

"I'm going to give you to Agent Rawlings. I'm driving at the moment." Beth handed her phone off to me. "I don't like to talk and drive without my Bluetooth," she said. "It's Agent Andrews."

I nodded and took the phone.

"This is Rawlings," I said.

"Hey, it's Andrews. I just got off the phone with Rebecca Wright's mother."

"Okay. Get something?" I asked.

"A couple of things. First, her vehicle isn't accounted for. I'm going to get an alert put out on the tags. I did the same with Kennedy Taylor's vehicle. The more important bit I got was that her mother said she was going to meet with a guy for coffee on Friday during lunch. Her mother spoke with her Friday morning. It was the last time the two talked."

I rested Beth's phone on my shoulder and pulled my notepad from my inner suit-jacket pocket to jot down what Andrews was telling me. "Define 'met with a guy for coffee.' Was this a lunch date? Did she know him? Do we have a name?" I asked.

"Everything I asked her mother. From what I got, she'd spoken with this guy—named John, no last name—online a number of times and then planned to meet with him on her lunch break from work. She worked in Skokie."

I wrote that down. "Where is that?" I asked.

"Northern Chicago suburb. I called her employer. She did return to work from her lunch break."

"Do we have a name of where they went to get

coffee?" I asked.

"No. But her lunch break was an hour, and she was back on time. That tells me that the furthest she could have probably traveled from work would be about twenty minutes, I'm giving it about a five-mile radius at the most. I'm sure you've noticed by now that driving ten miles anywhere in the Chicago area takes forty minutes."

I thought about it for a moment, and he was right.

Beth slowed for a yellow light that Ricodati, in his cruiser a few lengths ahead of us, had made. He pulled to the curb ahead and waited for the light to change so we could catch up.

I glanced out my window to see a coffee shop on the corner. I thought about the one right in front of our hotel and the countless others I'd seen, and I let out a breath. "That's literally got to be hundreds of places."

"Well, I didn't say that there wasn't going to be legwork involved, but it could be our best lead. I'm having my guys pull up and contact every coffee shop in that area. Her lunch break was at one p.m., so we should have a pretty good time frame to look into."

I wrote down the time she'd taken lunch. "This is all provided that she actually met with the guy we are searching for."

"True. I also already put in for her bank records to see if we can get a charge to a coffee shop."

"Okay. Did her mother mention how exactly she'd met this guy, other than online?"

"She didn't know. I asked. But she gave me a few phone numbers for friends that are on my to-call list. I'm going to try to knock those out before I leave for the evening."

The light turned green and Beth started forward. Ricodati pulled from the curb ahead to continue leading us.

"Okay. Keep me updated on that. When we get back to the hotel after viewing these dump sites, I'll get into the bank records from the prior victims. Maybe there is a coffee shop charge in those."

"Sure. I've been through them and don't necessarily remember any, but it's worth a second look," Andrews said. "Did you guys get anything on your end?"

"Right now, we're on our way to view the two sites out by the airport. We'll see if we get anything there. Aside from that, our supervisor back in Manassas got in contact with a few people at Classified OD."

Andrews interrupted. "Classified OD?"

"There's a chance that is how these women were in contact with our killer. We're meeting with a friend of Jasmine Thomas tomorrow. She's going to go on record that Jasmine met a man through the personals section of the site. We also have the sister of Kennedy Taylor saying that Kennedy met a man through that site, but she can't swear to it. We're thinking there is something there. I wanted to get the information from the website to see if, in fact, all the women were members and also the transcripts of their messages if they were. If we have a similar person they were all in contact with, well, that's probably our guy. Right now, it doesn't look like we have enough to get the proper legal docs to get them to release the information to us until we get that sworn statement."

"And they won't give us anything voluntarily, I'm assuming."

"Right. Someone from their legal team called our

supervisor back and told him they'd need subpoenas."

"Okay. You know they have an office here in Chicago, right?"

"They do?" I asked.

"It might actually be the headquarters. I'll look into it," Andrews said. "Let me get on making these calls. I'll see if the classified site rings any bells with any of her friends."

"Sure, let me know."

"Yup. I'll be in touch," Andrews said.

I clicked Beth's phone off and handed it back to her.

"What did he say?"

I gave her the highlights from my notes. "He spoke with the mother of the victim that was found this morning. She said her daughter, Rebecca, met with someone for coffee the Friday before she was found deceased. He has his guys looking into coffee shops around her workplace. I guess she did this on lunch and returned back to work. Aside from that, he has a list of her friends that he is going to try to make contact with."

"Where did she work?" Beth asked.

"Skokie. He didn't give the business name."

"We need to find out and get in contact with her employer. Maybe she came back to work with a cup of coffee from the place. Maybe it's in a garbage can next to her desk. Maybe the man she met with bought it for her and his prints are on it."

Beth had a number of plausible points. "Let me call Andrews back," I said.

CHAPTER TWENTY

We didn't get back to the hotel until after ten o'clock. Both crime scenes were in low-traffic areas of town, and aside from staring at Dumpsters and hearing Ricodati rehash how the two investigations had played out, we found nothing new. Andrews gave us Rebecca Wright's employer, the public works office for the city. We wouldn't be able to get into the building or meet with anyone until the next morning—our Thursday was quickly filling up with interviews and places we had to stop at. We put together a schedule, and Beth headed off to her room. I figured she was calling it a night.

I sat in the office chair at the small desk in my room and dialed Karen, having just finished making myself an eighteen-dollar gin and tonic.

"Hey, hon," she said.

"Hey. Sorry I didn't call sooner. We actually just got back to the hotel a little bit ago."

"That's a long day," she said.

"A long day of not really getting anywhere. Ah, I shouldn't say that. I guess we know a little more than when we got here and have a couple of guys working on a few things. It just seems like a hell of a lot of running around for not much. Interview after interview, meeting after meeting."

"Sorry," she said. "Maybe that's the job."

"What do you mean?"

"Just that whoever is doing this hasn't been caught by the local police or the FBI for years, right?"

"Right," I said.

"Well, if you're getting anywhere, I'd say that's a good thing."

Leave it to Karen to nail the voice-of-reason role.

"I guess you're right," I said.

"I take it you're done for the night?"

"Um, I might poke around at these bank records we have on the victims. I just want to see if I can find one thing specifically. After that, I'm shutting it down until tomorrow. I have another meeting with a family member at ten in the morning. Are you getting ready for bed?" I asked.

"I'm in bed. Watching television. Chop is lying next to me, slobbering up your pillow."

I smiled. "Great."

"Call me in the morning," she said.

"Okay. Love you."

"I love you too. Have a good night."

"You too. Bye." I hung up and tossed my phone onto the desk. Then I opened the file box of the victim's records and started thumbing through the folder containing the banking information from Kennedy Taylor.

A shave-and-a-haircut knock came at my room door. I walked over and opened it up.

"Two bits," I said.

Beth stood in the hall, looking back at me, confused. She wore a T-shirt and what looked like pajama pants. Her hair was no longer pulled up but resting on her shoulders. She wore a pair of dark-rimmed glasses.

"Shave and a haircut," I said.

Her face said she still didn't get it.

"Forget it." I motioned to her glasses. "Nice goggles," I said.

She smirked. "Oh, yeah, I took my contacts out. What's up with those banking records? Are you planning on going through them or are you done for the night?" she asked.

"I actually just started looking through them," I said.

"Want me to come in and lend a hand?" she asked. "Otherwise, you could just give me one or two of the girls, and I'll take them back to my room and go over them there if you wanted some private time or something."

I stepped to the side and waved her in. She walked to the box on the desk, grabbed a file, and went to the wingback chair. She sat, placed the folder on her lap, and opened it. She looked up at me. "How far into these did you get?"

"Just started on Kennedy Taylor," I said. I headed back over to the desk and sat down. "Keep your eyes peeled for coffee shops," I said.

"I'm actually just going to write down all purchases that aren't bills. You should do the same. Maybe we can match something up," Beth said.

"Good idea."

I took a sip from my drink and continued reading through the banking records. From all appearances,

Kennedy had been pretty smart with her money. The records went back five months. I didn't find any frivolous spending. Most of the activity was deposits—every few days. Her checking account balance seemed to hover around ten thousand, and it looked as though she made regular transfers to a savings account. My assumption, from what her parents had said, was that the savings account was where she was keeping the money she was saving for a house. It looked as though her only semiregular purchases were from a gas station near her house—they all seemed to be around forty dollars, so my best guess was that she was filling up her car with fuel. Through five months of records, she'd only made five or six purchases with her debit card that I'd wrote down.

"Kennedy Taylor worked in a restaurant, right?" I asked.

"Yeah, a place called The Pub if memory serves," Beth said.

"Okay. I'm almost through with her records here. She didn't use her debit card for much of anything, but working in a restaurant and getting tips would account for that, I guess."

"What do you mean?"

"Just that she'd always have cash on her."

Beth nodded.

"Well, for someone with not a lot of money, Jasmine sure liked to spend it. Not that there are any significant charges here, but she used her debit card about five times a day. This is going to take a bit." Beth adjusted her glasses on her nose. "She charged things for less than a dollar."

"Some people are like that. They just don't carry cash."

"I guess," Beth said. "Seems a little extreme, though. I

mean, if she took sixty dollars out of the bank a week, she would have been able to cover all these little charges."

I shrugged and reached into the box for the banking records on Angela Wormack. "See any charges from a coffee shop?"

"No."

I set Angela's banking file before me and started in. Beth's phone buzzed from across the room.

"Who is calling me this late?" she asked.

I didn't respond but turned to see Beth staring at the screen on her phone.

"Local number." Beth swiped the screen on her phone to answer. "Agent Beth Harper."

I couldn't hear who was on the other end.

"Yes, what did you get?"

Beth reached for the pad of paper and pen on the table next to her and jotted down a few things. "Really? What a coincidence." She gnawed on the end of her pen while she listened to the caller.

"Yeah, I would think that'd be enough to persuade someone to give us the rest," she said. "Okay, I'll let Hank know. We'll talk in the morning. Thanks for the call." Beth hung up.

"What was that?" I asked.

"Andrews. He just wrapped up a call with one of Rebecca Wright's friends. Rebecca met the guy she was going to get coffee with on Classified OD."

"Well, that takes care of that. It has to be our connection."

"It looks like it. He's going to meet this woman, Amy Meadows, now and get a sworn statement from her."

"He's meeting her this late?" I asked.

"He said she works at a bar or something and could take a break to meet with him."

"Okay, and then what?"

"As soon as he gets that, he'll be able to get a subpoena for her transcripts from the website," she said. "With her statement and the one we get for Jasmine Thomas, it should be enough probable cause for us to secure subpoenas for all of the women, I would think."

"Perfect. About time we're getting somewhere."

"This is actually moving along a hell of a lot faster than normal. Usually, things don't go this way. Leads in these investigations are few and far between for the most part. I'm thinking we're going to get this guy."

"Hopefully before he kills anyone else," I said.

Beth nodded.

CHAPTER TWENTY-ONE

Brett drove Rebecca's couple-year-old Honda toward Aurora, a city forty-five minutes northwest of his house. He wore dark clothes, a baseball cap, and thin black leather gloves. Beneath him, covering the seat was plastic sheeting that he would take with him when he left the car. He had a reason for choosing that town, something he'd stumbled upon when he was going through Monica's correspondences from the website just before he deleted them. Brett had spotted a user name that looked familiar—it was a user name he'd seen while looking into everyone Rebecca had chatted with. He reinstated both women's accounts to confirm.

Monica and Becca had apparently both been speaking with another man—the same man. He went by the handle of Ladykiller75. His real name was Jeff Mercer. Brett had gotten his IP address and found him. The user name couldn't have been more perfect.

If the feds were in fact sniffing into the women and had figured out that they'd all used his site, they would have a number-one suspect in Mr. Mercer. Furthermore, when they found the body of one woman he'd spoken with—along with the vehicle of another—near his home, that would really tip the scales. Brett had reinstated each woman's messages through the website, all except the ones he'd sent and received.

Brett exited the highway and traveled the city streets, looking for the perfect place to be rid of her. Once he left Becca's car and Monica's body, he would walk a mile or two until he found a bar. From there, he'd call a number of taxis with his prepaid phone to get back home. He had a pocket full of cash to pay the drivers and a number of random addresses he would have them drop him off at.

The clock on the dash read a few minutes after midnight. The area was quiet, as it should have been. He spotted an old church next to what looked like a small single-story factory on his right—that would make a suitable place to leave her.

Brett slowed and made the turn onto the small road that split the church and the business. A dead end sign stood on the right-hand side of the street between the road and the factory's parking lot. Brett glanced left to see a small building and a single light on a pole behind the church. To his right, a handful of cars were parked in the well-lit factory parking lot, and beyond the cars were more parking spots and a row of green Dumpsters. Brett didn't plan on removing Monica from the trunk—he assumed that within a day or two, the car would be called in and the plates would be run and would lead back to Becca, who they knew was murdered. The police would search the car and find Monica's body.

Brett pulled past both the church and the factory and killed the car's headlights as he approached the end of the street. Then he pulled the car to the right side of the road and stopped at the metal barrier and dead end sign that wouldn't allow him to go any further. Brett left the keys in the ignition, opened the door, stepped out, and pulled the plastic from the driver's seat. He closed the door and looked around, spotting no one.

Brett balled up the plastic sheeting and headed for the row of Dumpsters by the factory to toss it. He kept a watchful eye on his surroundings as he entered the factory's lighted parking lot. He spotted the business name on a sign on the side of the building: Penn's Tool and Die. Brett walked to the second Dumpster and lifted the lid just enough to toss the plastic inside. He let the lid fall and took a step back toward the street.

"What did you just toss in there?" a voice asked.

Brett froze. He slowly turned his head to the right to look at the back of the factory. He saw the glow of fire from the end of a cigarette and the silhouette of a man behind it, leaning against the back of the building.

"Some garbage from the car," Brett said.

"You know that's illegal, right?" the man asked. "What are you doing back here anyway?"

"Just had to take a piss," Brett said. He continued walking.

"Also illegal," the voice said.

Brett didn't turn back to look at the guy. "Yeah, just mind your own business, buddy." He walked back toward the car—he needed to look elsewhere for a place to dump it and the girl.

"Kind of warm for gloves isn't it?" the guy asked. "What are you up to?"

He stopped walking and turned toward the guy, who

was standing at the Dumpster, peering under the lid to see what Brett had tossed.

Brett figured he'd try a story to defuse the situation. "Look, man, I was at the bar. Some girl gave me her address to come over. I'm not from around here and am lost. Sorry—I stopped, took a piss, and tossed something in your Dumpster. Geez. I'm not out here hurting anybody, man."

The guy let out a breath. "Where are you trying to go? Do you have the address?"

This guy isn't going to let up.

"Yeah, I have it on a piece of paper." Brett fished around in his pocket and started walking toward the guy, who was still standing at the Dumpster. The lights from the parking lot lit the guy up. He wore a green oil-stained T-shirt and a pair of dirty jeans. The man looked to be in his fifties, with stringy chin-length hair. Brett had him by a good thirty pounds. The cigarette the man smoked hung from his mouth.

When Brett was within a few feet, the guy held out his hand for Brett to hand him the address. Brett took another step toward the man, swatted his hand away and delivered a walking forearm to the guy's face. Sparks from the cigarette's cherry filled the air. The guy reached for his nose. Brett delivered another forearm, connecting with the tip of his elbow to the man's temple over his raised arms. The man dropped to a knee. Brett grabbed him by the back of the hair, lifted him back to his feet, and smashed his face into the top edge of the Dumpster. He pulled the man's head back and slammed it into the metal edge again—and again. Finally, Brett let go. The man collapsed to the ground, not moving. Brett couldn't take a chance that the man would live and be able to identify him, so he pulled the man to the back side of the Dumpsters, knelt next to him, and wrapped his gloved hands around the guy's throat. Then Brett squeezed as hard as he could and held the position for minutes. He eventually let go. The man was dead. Brett popped his head up over the top of the Dumpster and looked back toward the factory—he saw no one outside.

Brett casually walked into the darkness beyond the dead end sign at the end of the street.

CHAPTER TWENTY-TWO

I woke to rapid pounding on the door of my hotel room. I squinted hard and cracked my eyes open. The red LED time on the alarm clock sitting on the nightstand next to the bed blurred and then came into focus—5:57 a.m. The person knocking had to be Beth.

"One second," I yelled.

I flipped the sheets back and climbed from bed. I pulled on my pants, lying at the side of the bed, and tossed on my shirt from the day prior. I walked to the door, looked through the peephole, and pulled the room door open. I rubbed my eyes with my thumb and index finger. Beth stood before me in the hall, wearing her same pajama pants and T-shirt from the night before.

"What's up?" I asked.

"Come on, get ready. We have to go."

"For what? It's six in the morning."

"You didn't hear your phone ringing?"

"No," I said.

"Okay, well, rise and shine, and get your ass ready. We have multiple bodies."

"Multiple bodies?" I asked.

"I'll tell you on the way. We're leaving in fifteen."

I nodded and closed the door. I walked to my phone and removed it from the charger—it showed three missed calls and three voice mails. I clicked the button to hear them. All three were from Andrews and within the last twenty minutes. The first said he'd gotten a call from his field office that they'd found a murdered man and Rebecca Wright's car in Aurora. The second message confirmed the first and added that they'd also found a deceased woman. The third message said he was en route to the scene and we should meet him there as soon as possible. I deleted the messages and headed for the bathroom to get ready.

I started the shower and brushed my teeth, staring at myself in the mirror. My eyes were puffed up from lack of sleep, and black stubble, with a little silver mixed in, filled my cheeks and chin. I didn't have time for a shave. I quickly showered and dressed in the last clean suit hanging in the closet. Beth was once again banging on my door within a minute of me getting ready. I pulled the room door open. She stepped in, dressed, her brown hair tied back, and ready to go to work.

"I just called for the car. Are you ready?" she asked.

"Think so," I said.

"Well, grab whatever you'll need for the day, I'm not sure if we'll be back before tonight."

I nodded, rubbed my eyes again, and walked to my desk. I grabbed everything I saw. My brain was still a little slow at functioning to remember what my exact schedule for the day was and precisely what I'd need.

I tucked the files under my arm and followed Beth

from the room toward the elevators. She thumbed the button to take us down.

"Where is Aurora?" I asked.

"An hour drive west."

"I listened to Andrew's messages. They found Rebecca Wright's car, another woman, and a man?"

The elevator doors opened. We stepped inside and hit the button for the lobby.

"I talked to him briefly," she said. "That's the gist of what he told me."

"Do we have an ID on either of the deceased?" I asked.

"He didn't say. The local PD was leaving the scene as is until the FBI arrived. Andrews should be getting there soon. He said forty-five minutes when I talked to him twenty minutes or so ago."

I nodded.

The elevator doors opened, letting us into the lobby. We walked through and outside. Beth's car hadn't arrived.

She jerked her head toward a woman leaning out the door of the coffee shop next to where we stood. "Looks like they are just opening. Why don't you grab us two coffees and something that would qualify as breakfast. Muffin or something."

I wouldn't argue. A coffee was a necessity after the four hours of sleep I'd had.

"What do you want in it?" I asked.

"Lots of sugar. Lots of cream," she said.

"Right, so chocolate milk?" I asked.

She rolled her eyes.

I headed into the coffee shop, grabbed two tall cups and a couple of muffins, and headed back outside. Beth was waiting in front of the hotel in her car. I walked over, set what I was carrying on the roof and opened the door. I handed Beth's coffee to her, grabbed the rest of the stuff from the roof, and got in. She pulled away from the curb.

"So the local PD there called the FBI?" I asked.

"I didn't get the whole story of how it went down or what exactly is going on out there," Beth said. "Andrews just said they found the car, we had another, and then mentioned there was a deceased man as well. I asked what was up with the deceased man, but he said he didn't know."

"I guess we'll see shortly," I said.

"How late did you stay up?" Beth asked.

"Until around two. Once I finished up with the bank records, I moved on to the phone records."

"Anything?"

I shook my head. "Nothing that stood out. Did you grab the schedule we put together for today?"

"Um, yeah, it's in the bag back there." Beth pointed over her shoulder to a leather business bag in the back seat. "What do you need to know?"

"What we have for today. I was half awake when we were leaving. I'm thinking maybe we should have taken two cars."

"I thought about it. We should be fine unless this takes more than two hours. We'll probably have to leave Aurora by nine to meet with Andrea Fradet at ten. We need her sworn statement. That's the most important thing right now. After that, we'll need to go to the local FBI field office. We should be able to get everything filed in order to get a subpoena, as well as check in with the tech-department guys to see if they came up with anything from the computer or tablet. Who knows, maybe they just weren't able to get to it yet."

"You never heard anything back from them?"

"Nope."

"I would imagine you would have, one way or the other, if they got to them. Did we still plan to go out to Skokie, look around, and have some talks with the coworkers of Rebecca Wright?" I asked.

"I think we should."

I pulled out my notepad and started jotting a few things down.

"What are you writing?" Beth asked.

"We haven't met with anyone regarding Rebecca Wright. I'm just making myself a note to see what exactly Andrews got and to get a copy of everything he's collected on her. I think we should introduce ourselves to her family and let them know we are working with Andrews on it," I said.

"It's a good idea."

She reached out and powered on the car stereo. The volume was faint, yet it sounded like some early-morning talk radio. I caught the words "women" and "bodies" almost immediately, so I reached out and turned the volume up. The host of the radio show was talking about our investigation. He said something along the lines of "How many bodies have to turn up before law enforcement connects the dots?" He went on to say that he wasn't a detective, and he was sure that the authorities were trying, but the body count was rising with no end in sight. I turned the volume back down.

"Sounds like the same things the local news is saying," Beth said.

"I haven't been watching," I said. "No time."

"Well, it's been getting pretty bad. I had the news on before I went to sleep last night. When word hits of this new victim, things are only going to get worse."

"What are the local stations saying?"

"They are doing their best to make everyone in the city scared, splashing the words 'serial killer' all over," Beth said. "Things like local law enforcement has no answers, authorities at a loss, no suspects, and stuff like that. It makes relations with the families worse when the media spins everyone up. Plus, I'm sure the local branch of the FBI is being pressured from all the attention the investigation is getting. I'm guessing that was why Agent Andrews was making midnight statement runs last night."

I nodded. "You're probably right. Okay, well, we're going to need to get all of our information in order today or tonight. We'll talk with Andrews, contact each family, and try to get something together for some kind of a press conference," I said. "We need to let the public know that this is being taken seriously and we are doing all we can."

"I'm not good on camera," Beth said. "I freeze up and stumble. Fear of speaking in public, I think it's called."

"I'll take care of it," I said.

CHAPTER TWENTY-THREE

Beth and I arrived on the scene around a quarter after seven. A black Aurora patrol car with a single white door and insignia was blocking the entrance to a dead-end street. An officer stood near the trunk. Beth turned the nose of the car toward the police cruiser and stopped. The officer approached.

"Street is closed, ma'am," he said.

Beyond him and his car were more patrol cars and a black government-issue Crown Victoria sedan parked in the lot of a tool-and-die factory to the right.

Beth showed the patrol officer her credentials. "We're with the other FBI agent here."

He nodded and moved his car so we could pull through.

To our left was a small church looking as if it had been built in the early nineteen hundreds. A small home matching the style of the church stood behind it. Straight ahead of us, at the end of the dead-end street, was a maroon Honda Accord with the trunk open. A few officers stood at the back of it. A coroner's van was parked to the Accord's left.

Beth drove the short street to the end and turned right into the factory's entrance. A row of green Dumpsters lined the back of the parking lot to our left, with more police officers standing nearby. We spotted Agent Andrews resting his arms on the roof of his car, speaking on his telephone. Beth parked next to his black Crown Victoria, and we stepped out. I took a minute to look at the factory—it was a small flat-roofed single-story cinderblock building. Above the single entrance door was a rectangular metal sign reading Penn's Tool and Die.

Andrews clicked off from his phone call and slipped his phone into his pocket. "This is bad," he said.

We walked to him.

"What do we have?" I asked.

He waved over his shoulder for Beth and me to follow him. "It's ugly. The man is over here behind the Dumpsters."

Neither Beth nor I said anything as we followed Andrews. He walked to the front side of the row of Dumpsters, stopped a few feet short, and pointed down at what looked like a large blood pool and drag marks. "This is where it started," he said.

"This is from the man?" I asked.

"Yeah," Andrews said.

I looked down at the pool and back up at the edge of the Dumpster, also covered in blood. I noticed a pair of officers and another man standing just on the other side.

Andrews waved us to continue following him. "Looks like drag marks leading around to the backside of the Dumpsters here." Andrews rounded the corner pointing down.

He walked toward the two officers and the coroner—judging by the patch on his jacket—standing next to a body covered in a yellow plastic tarp.

Andrews stopped near the men. "This is Agents Rawlings and Harper," he said.

The two officers nodded but said nothing.

I caught the name plates on their shirts, Garlington and Rae.

"We think that he saw the guy dumping the woman and car," said the one on the left, Garlington. He scratched at the front of his dark hairline, which formed a widow's peak.

I turned my attention to him. He looked to be early thirties, slim, and an inch or two under six foot. He and his partner both wore all-black uniforms with a yellow-and-navy eagle patch on the shoulder.

"Who was he?" Beth asked.

"Third-shift employee from the tool-and-die factory there," said the other officer, Rae. He jerked his chin toward the building. The officer looked to be a few years older than the other and quite a bit shorter, probably five six. A pair of dark plastic sunglasses rested on his forehead, and a faint trace of a mustache sat on his upper lip. "His name was Ted Biller," Rae said.

"What do we know?" I asked.

"The guy went out for a smoke and never came back," Andrews said. "After about a half hour, another employee, waiting on parts from this guy, came out looking for him. He didn't find him but noticed his car was still there. After another hour or so, a different employee came out for a cigarette and went to toss his empty pack in the Dumpster. He saw all the blood, followed the smear

marks back around the row of Dumpsters, and saw this."
He pointed at the body.

I stepped around the body and motioned for the
coroner to lift the tarp. He knelt and raised the corner.
The victim lay on his back, facing the sky. His nose looked
to be broken, the left side of his face crushed. Most of
what I could see was covered in blood.

"C.O.D.?" I asked.

"Bruising on the neck is consistent with strangulation,"
the coroner said. "Yet I think the injuries to the head may
have been enough."

"We may have skin under his nails if this was a
strangulation," Beth said.

"My forensics team is on the way. That's why the
bodies haven't been removed," Andrews said.

I motioned for the coroner to replace the tarp.
"Where's the woman?" I asked.

Andrews pointed toward the car and began walking.
Beth and I followed. As we neared the back of the maroon
Honda, I caught a faint smell of death—from experience,
I knew bodies didn't start to smell until they'd been dead
for a full day. This one had been killed far earlier than the
man. The two patrol officers standing near the rear of the
car walked away. Andrews stopped at the trunk and
pointed inside.

I looked in. A dead woman with long dark hair lay
inside. Her hair covered most of her face except her foggy
right eye, which seemed to be focused on me. My eyes
went to her arms, looking for needle marks—they were
present. The woman wore a small white dress with thin
straps at the top and a matching pair of white high heels.
She looked ready for a night on the town.

"Poor girl," Beth said.

"Who is it?" I asked.

"Monica Whickham," Andrews said. "Patrol pulled an ID from her purse there." He nodded toward the purse lying beside the dead woman.

"And the car belongs to Rebecca Wright?" Beth asked.

"Correct," Andrews said.

"How did they find her in the trunk?" Beth asked.

"Local PD got a call from the factory about the man. When they arrived on scene, they saw the car here and ran the plates—came back to Rebecca Wright with a note that I had put on the tags to immediately contact myself at the Chicago FBI. It's how I was alerted so fast. I guess a few of the employees inside said that the car wasn't there prior to them starting their shift, meaning it was left there within an hour or two of the murder happening. The patrol guys went back to the car and had a better look around, which was when one of the officers saw the keys in the ignition. They went through the car, found the girl."

"So where did our killer go?" I asked. "And was he planning on leaving Rebecca Wright's car here?"

"Good question," Beth said.

"The guy could be local to the area," Andrews said.

The noise of tires coming down the short street caught my ear. I turned to look and saw a black van with another black Crown Victoria following it.

"That's going to be our forensics unit and Agent Toms," Andrews said.

I nodded.

The two vehicles pulled into the parking lot and stopped. The forensics team stepped from the van.

I turned my attention back to Andrews. "So what are

we thinking went down here?"

"My take on it…" Andrews paused. "Our guy drove back into this dead-end street to dump the girl's body in one of the Dumpsters, got seen, killed the witness, and just left everything behind."

It made sense from what I'd just looked at. I caught another whiff of the body, which made the coffee and muffin in my stomach turn. One would think I would've built a tolerance for the smell from years of working homicide and smelling dead bodies. I hadn't. I rubbed my nose and tried to limit the air I was taking in. "You said the local PD went through the car?" I asked.

"They didn't print it or anything. Waiting on my guys," Andrews said.

I nodded and headed toward the driver's door, and Beth followed. Andrews met the forensics unit and Agent Toms at the trunk of the car.

"We have about an hour or so before we have to head out to make that meeting on time," Beth said. "I think I'm going to go do a little questioning with the employees. I want to get the timeline nailed down here."

"Sure," I said.

Beth walked toward the entrance of the factory while I stayed put and stared through the driver's-side window of the car, looking for anything of interest. Something protruding from halfway under the passenger seat caught my eye almost immediately—the bottom edge of a brown disposable coffee cup.

"Andrews," I called.

He came from the trunk area to my side.

"What's up?" he asked.

"Have one of your guys grab that." I pointed toward

the passenger-side floor.

Andrews looked over my shoulder through the window of the car. "Reese, are you gloved up?" he asked.

One of the forensics guys from the trunk area responded yes.

"Open the passenger side and get that cup from the floor," Andrews said.

The man walked to the passenger side, pulled the door open, and reached in. He grabbed the bottom corner of the cup with his gloved fingertips and removed it from the car. The disposable cup had a white plastic top and a cardboard sleeve. "Empty coffee cup." He looked at the top. "Lipstick on the rim." He headed for the trunk.

Andrews and I met him at the back.

"Let me get this in a bag," Reese said. He knelt, reached into his kit, and pulled a clear evidence bag out. He dropped the cup in and held it up before Andrews and me.

I stared at the cardboard sleeve wrapping the cup halfway up. "Bean Grinders Inc. Where is that?"

"I'm looking," Andrews said. He held his phone in his hand, searching the location of the coffee shop. Andrews looked at me. "It's about a quarter mile outside of the radius I had my guys searching. I'm going to give this scene to Toms and go check out the coffee shop."

"One second," I said. "What's going on with your subpoena?"

"It should be at the office. I haven't even gone in yet this morning."

"How is it being served?"

"Their legal department is downtown. I'm walking it in and leaving with the information in my hand," Andrews said.

I thought for a moment. We needed to meet with Andrea Fradet in order to get the sworn statement to get another subpoena. Beth believed having two would be enough to secure subpoenas on each victim. We could get all the information and transcripts from Classified OD in one shot. "Let me make a call quick," I said.

I pulled my phone and dialed Ball. He answered within a couple rings.

"Ball," he said.

"It's Rawlings."

"I'm just waking up. What's going on?"

"Another victim and a deceased male that we believe could have been a witness to the body dump."

Ball didn't immediately respond.

I continued. "What I need to know is if we have two sworn statements stating that the victims were using the classified site, is that enough to get a subpoena for them to release all the victim's information to us? That is, if they have it."

"Two can still be a coincidence. It will end up being a judgment call by whoever is issuing the subpoenas. Three or four, and well, that's a different story. If you want my opinion, take what you have this second and run with it."

"All right, I'll call you back in a bit and fill you in on this scene and where we're at."

"Okay," Ball said.

I hung up.

"Supervisor?" Andrews asked.

"Yeah. Shit, I should have driven myself."

"Well, what do you need?"

"Ball, my superior in Manassas says take what we have this second and run, meaning if that subpoena is back at the office, it should be served as soon as possible. I'm damn near positive that whatever information we get from Classified OD will lead us to whoever is behind this. I'll see if Beth can take the meeting with Jasmine Thomas's friend solo. If she can do that and you can get the subpoena taken care of, I can get dropped at my hotel, get my car, and check out the coffee shop."

"I'm good with that," he said.

"Okay, so you have to go to the Chicago office to get the subpoena, correct?"

"Correct."

"What time do your tech guys show up?" I asked.

"About eight."

"Can you make sure they get on that tablet, specifically, as soon as they get in?" I asked. "It's Kennedy Taylor's. We need to see if there is anything on it connecting her to the classified site."

"I'll make sure it's the first thing they do."

"Okay. Beth will have to go back to the Chicago office when she's done in order to get the second subpoena. I'll meet her there when I'm done at the coffee shop. I'll give you a call when we're both there if you're not back."

"Sounds good. I'm going to find Toms and let him know this is his scene."

I nodded and headed for the factory to find Beth.

CHAPTER TWENTY-FOUR

Brett sat in front of his computer. Though he'd showered and drunk multiple cups of coffee, it had done nothing to lift him from his sleep-deprived state. From Aurora, he'd taken five cab rides, waiting between a half hour and an hour between each pickup. The final ride dropped him two miles from his house, and he walked the rest of the way. The total trip had taken him the better part of seven hours—the travel time gave him hours to think. Brett had decided that he was done for a bit—the need fulfilled for the time being. The killing of the man was messy, and the thought of feds sniffing around was unsettling.

Brett dug his fingers into his eyes and gave them a hard rub. He needed to get his focus.

Brett let out a long breath and accessed his website's system files to begin the process of deleting anything related to him. The moment he logged in, he noticed a message alert at the top of the screen. He clicked on it.

The message read: *Hey Tom. Been a while. I wanted to see if maybe you wanted to have lunch this week. -Mandy*

The corner of Brett's mouth rose into a smirk. He'd

taken the woman out for coffee prior to killing Angela Wormack. When Brett tried contacting her again, she never responded. He'd logged into the website's message system and saw she was in regular contact with another man. The two had sent each other dozens of messages a day, talking about dates they'd gone out on, enjoying time with each other, and things of that nature.

"Looks like her budding relationship went south," Brett said.

He scratched at his chin. The decision came quickly— he would leave it to chance.

Brett typed: *Love to, give me a call.*

He included the number of the prepaid phone he'd used to call the taxis. If she called, she would die. If she didn't, she would live.

Brett continued deleting everything related to him across the website. Each different version of his personals ad—gone. Every message he'd ever sent to anyone—gone. The profile he'd used—gone. Any record of his user name—gone.

Brett logged out of the website's system files and left his home office. He needed to get to work.

CHAPTER TWENTY-FIVE

Beth had dropped me at the hotel a half hour prior and headed out toward Shaumburg to meet with Andrea Fradet. Since I was going to be in the general area of Skokie, I planned to check out Rebecca Wright's workplace and speak with some coworkers when I was through with checking out the coffee shop.

My cell phone's navigation said I was nearing Bean Grinders Inc., driving north on Waukegan Road. The beacon on the app told me the address was on the right before the next main street. I saw the crossroad in the distance but didn't see any street parking. To my right was a long three-story brick building. I was approaching an entrance that went under the building, where a sign read Public Parking. I slowed from the speed limit to check it out. Businesses were taking up the first floor, and I assumed apartments sat on the two stories above the stores. The sound of a horn startled me. I glanced into the rearview mirror to see the grille of a pickup truck a few feet from the back of my rental. I clicked on my directional to pull into the parking area. The truck following veered around me, and I glanced at him as he passed. The guy waved his hands in the air and yelled what sounded like "Learn how to drive."

I shrugged it off and pulled under the building. What I'd assumed was a parking structure wasn't. After going under the apartments overhead, the entrance turned to the left and led to an outdoor parking lot behind the building. I found a spot, grabbed the file I'd brought, and stepped out. I glanced at the screen of my phone one more time and turned off the navigation. I walked back around the complex the way I'd pulled in and found the coffee shop at the end of the row of businesses on the corner. I looked past the outdoor seating and through the windows as I neared the front door. The place was small, but all the seats were full. A huge banner across the window claimed Chicagoland's Best Coffee.

I pulled the front door open to the sounds of bells attached to the doorframe and made my way to the front counter.

A young woman looked at me with a smile. "What can I get for you? We're running a two-for-one on baked goods."

"I actually need to see the manager or owner," I said.

"Um, okay. Give me just a second, and I'll get Vanessa."

"Thank you."

I stepped from the counter and looked over the offerings of coffee and coffee cups for sale while I waited. A coffee cup that said BOSS on it caught my eye. I picked it up, gave it a look, and smiled. I set it back down and continued browsing. A moment later, I noticed the girl I'd spoken with pointing at me from behind the counter while another woman, a bit heavyset, stood next to her. The heavyset woman approached. Her black hair was pulled back in a ponytail. She wore a tan apron over a black long-sleeved blouse. I put her in her early thirties.

"I'm Vanessa, the owner. How can I help you?"

I glanced left and right at the customers in the shop—at least five people within earshot. I reached into my pocket, pulled my credentials, and flashed them to her. "Do you have an office?" I asked.

She looked confused but nodded and waved me behind the counter. I followed her as she turned right and entered a small office. She closed the door at my back. Miscellaneous bags of coffee, merchandise, and supplies filled the room, and the woman's desk was a mess. A computer monitor had what appeared to be some kind of financial spreadsheet open behind the desk. I didn't see a guest chair.

She rounded the desk and took a seat. "Sorry it's such a mess in here. It's the only room we have aside from the main area, so it kind of has to double as a storage room as well."

"No problem," I said. "I figured this would be a little better than trying to speak in front of your customers."

She nodded. "I have to say, I have no idea why the FBI would be here."

"We're conducting an investigation and found a coffee cup from here. We found it in the car that belonged to a victim of a homicide."

Her face looked troubled. "Oh my."

"Well," I continued, "we believe this victim met for coffee with a man prior to the crime being committed. We believe that that meeting could have very well been at your business here."

"Um, okay."

"Do you have video here, ma'am?"

She nodded. "We have a couple of cameras in the building."

"Would I be able to view some of that video?"

"Um, sure. When were you looking for?"

I reached into my suit jacket and pulled out my notepad. I flipped to the page where I'd taken notes from my phone call with Andrews. "Last Friday between one and two in the afternoon."

"Okay, it's going to take me a minute to pull this up. I'm not so hot with the video system."

"Sure," I said.

"Did you want to grab a coffee while you wait? On the house."

"I hear it's Chicago's best."

"That's not just a slogan. We've won awards."

"I should probably try it, then," I said.

"Just stick your head out of the door, ask, and Melony will bring you one."

I opened the office door, requested a cup of dark roast, black, and had it in hand moments later. I stepped back into the office and again stood watching the owner clicking keys on her computer. A moment later, video played on the monitor. I blew across the top of the coffee and took a sip. The coffee was exceptionally strong yet smooth—the best I'd had in quite a long time.

The owner, Vanessa, didn't take her eyes from the computer. "Well, how is it?"

"Excellent," I said.

A hint of a smile crossed her face and disappeared just as quickly.

The owner rolled her chair a foot back from the computer screen and waved me over. "Here we go. Friday at one o'clock."

I rounded the woman's desk and looked at the screen, which was divided into quarters. One camera was mounted on each counter, with two cameras for the indoor seating area. I opened my folder and pulled out the driver's license photo of Rebecca Wright. "This is the woman we're looking for."

She looked at the photo, nodded, and fast forwarded until someone approached the counter. We repeated the process for the first ten minutes then slowed to watch everyone in the business come, order, and sit or go in real time.

At seventeen minutes after one o'clock, a woman I figured to be Rebecca Wright appeared in the building. She walked to the counter, ordered, and paid cash. She stood around for another few minutes before taking her coffee and walking from the front of the building. We followed her in the corner of the screen through what the indoor camera caught of the outside seating area. Rebecca took a seat, alone, outside at the table next to the front door. A minute or two later, someone approached her. Rebecca stood and appeared to hug the person, who was mostly blocked out by the Chicagoland's Best Coffee banner. The person slid out a chair with his foot and took a seat on the other side of the table. All I could really see was that it appeared to be a male, he wore gray pants, and his hands were clasped together on the table's top. He appeared to be wearing a suit. The two sat for twenty minutes before Rebecca stood and appeared to hug the person again, and they both walked off. The man never entered the building and never had a coffee. I watched the guy's hands the entire time he sat at the table—he never touched anything.

"Shit," I said.

The owner glanced up at me standing over her, looking at the screen.

"Sorry," I said. "Do you think I could get a copy of this footage?"

She scrunched her face. "I don't actually know how to do that."

"How long does your system save video for?"

She shrugged. "Until it's full? I honestly don't know."

"Well, how long back can you access from today?"

She clicked a couple of keys and looked at me. "Looks like a month or so."

"Okay. I'm going to get someone in here who can make a copy of the footage if that's all right."

"That would be fine."

I thanked her for her time and purchased the BOSS coffee mug on my way out. I hopped into my rental car and dialed Beth, who answered right away.

"Good timing. I'm just about to walk up to the condo that this Andrea lives in. Did you come up with anything out there?"

"I have her on video meeting a guy."

"Great!" Beth said.

"Except the guy never enters the building, you can't see much of him or his body, he never orders a coffee, and the owner doesn't know how to make me a copy of the footage."

"Ugh," she said. "Not so great."

"Correct. Not so great."

"Can we get anything from it? Height, weight, hair color? Did you see the guy touch anything?"

"He didn't touch a single thing. The height, weight and hair I'm not sure on from the video I saw. I'll ask one of the tech guys back at the Chicago office if they can make a trip out here and copy the video either way, maybe they can do something with it."

"They should be able to at least copy it and look at it further," she said.

"That's what I was thinking."

"Are you heading over to Skokie to her employer now?" Beth asked.

"Yeah, I'm not sure if there is going to be anything for us there, but I'm in the neighborhood, and it's worth the trip, I guess."

"Okay. Let me get this interview done, and then I'll meet you back at the Chicago office."

"Sounds good," I said.

"See you in a bit." She hung up.

I searched for the Skokie public works office in my phone and hit the button to navigate to it. My phone informed me the drive would be just ten minutes. I followed the suggested route.

CHAPTER TWENTY-SIX

I flashed my credentials as I pulled into the Chicago FBI office. The stop at Rebecca Wright's employer had been less than fruitful. She'd worked in the records department with one other person sharing her office. The two women weren't close and didn't speak outside of work. Rebecca's supervisor allowed me to look around her desk—I didn't see anything out of the ordinary. I'd gotten in and out within forty-five minutes.

I found a parking spot in the lot and got out. I'd spoken with Andrews on the drive back. He was at the Classified OD office downtown, waiting to speak with someone in their legal department. He said he'd have Agent Toms meet me in the lobby and take me over to the tech department, who'd apparently found something. I tried calling Beth on my way back to the field office, but the call went to her voice mail—I'd assumed she was still conducting her interview with Andrea Fradet.

I entered the building and walked across the FBI insignia toward the desk near the back. The same security guard from the other day greeted me at the counter.

"Here for Agent Toms," I said.

"Ah, he wanted me to give him a jingle when you arrived. Um, Agent Rawlings, right?" he asked.

I nodded.

"Let me get him down here. One second."

I glanced at the guy's name badge—Jerry. He picked up the phone, made a call, and hung up a few seconds later.

"He'll be down in a second," Jerry said.

"Sure. Thanks." I leaned against the front counter and waited. I pulled back the sleeve on my suit jacket and checked the time—a few minutes after eleven. I pulled out my phone. I'd missed two calls from Karen in the last few hours. I sent her off a quick text message that I'd gotten an early start, loved her, and would call her as soon as I could.

The elevator doors at the side of the room opened, and Agent Toms headed my way.

"The tech guys found something for you, I hear," he said.

I turned to face him. "Yeah, that's what Andrews said. Know what they found?"

He shook his head, causing his jowls to wiggle. "Let's go find out. They are in the other building. Figured I'd walk you over there instead of having you come up, then down, then walk you over there."

"Fair enough."

Agent Toms headed toward the doors at the side of the building opposite the elevators. I followed him outside and into the adjacent building.

"Get anything else from out at that scene in Aurora?" I asked.

"I just got back a little bit ago. Left as soon as our forensics unit had finished with the bodies." He stopped in front of an elevator and thumbed the button to take us up. "Not sure if we got anything new, but the vehicle will be brought back to our garages here this afternoon for forensic processing. We have a few agents sticking around the area to do some door knocking, and Agent Bower, who I left the scene with, will touch base with the family as soon as they arrive at the medical examiner's."

"Okay. So the family of the woman has been contacted?"

The elevator doors opened, and we stepped inside. Toms pressed the button for the second floor. "The local medical examiner will contact the family for identification. After that, Agent Bower will introduce himself to the family, collect their contact information, and forward it on to Andrews, you, and your partner for interviews."

I nodded.

The elevator let us out on two. I followed Toms down the hall to the left. He stopped at a pair of frosted glass doors that simply said Technology Unit in black. He pushed the door open, and we entered. A large white-floored room spread out before us. Workstations and rows of computer monitors filled the right and left walls. Each workstation appeared to have a bank of six computer monitors dedicated to it, two monitors high by three wide. A gray rectangular desk ran directly down the center of the room, covered with more computer monitors, power ports, and what looked like diagnostic equipment. A man glanced over at us as he connected a laptop computer to a port on the desk's top. At the workstations on my left and right, four men and two women sat. Blue FBI jackets hung on the backs of a few of their office chairs. Toms walked toward the back of the room. The far wall we approached was white and filled with windows and doors. Through the windows, I could see that each room was an individual lab. Toms turned right at the back of the room, walked down a short hallway, and stopped at an office door. He rapped on the door with his knuckles and pulled it open when someone inside told him to come on in.

I entered the office behind Agent Toms. A man sat behind a desk, looking up at us. At his back was another wall of monitors in the same fashion as the workstations in the main office—two by three. The man had dark hair that receded in the front. He appeared in his late forties, and a graying goatee wrapped his mouth. He wore a blue dress shirt and patterned gray tie.

"Skip, this is Agent Rawlings," Toms said. "Rawlings, this is Skip Brady. He runs the tech unit here."

The man rose from his chair and shook my hand.

"From Virginia, right?" he asked.

I nodded. "I heard you guys found something on the computer and tablet that were dropped off," I said.

"Find something, we did," he said. "Let's go have a talk with my guy who found it."

He rounded his desk and waved for Agent Toms and me to follow him from his office.

We all walked the short hall back toward the labs. I looked through the lab window on my right and spotted the computer and tablet we'd brought in, sitting on the workstation there. A man was sitting in front of a computer in the corner of the lab, his back to us. Skip knocked on the door, and we entered. The man before the computer spun on his chair to face us. He appeared to be in his early thirties and was small in stature. He wore a yellow dress shirt, which looked a size too large, tucked into a pair of khakis, with a black tie.

"This is Mike O'Neil. He's got something for you on these electronics," Skip said.

I shook the guy's hand. "Agent Hank Rawlings."

"Pleasure," he said.

"So what did you find?"

"Well, I've been working with the Jasmine Thomas computer mostly because the tablet is cooked—more on that in a minute."

"Find anything on the computer?" I asked.

"Well, it works, and we have access to everything. I was left a note to be on the lookout for anything related to Classified OD. I tried looking into that. There was nothing in her browsing history related to the site, but we do have something interesting."

"What's that?"

"Well, Jasmine had one of these programs installed on her computer that remembers logins and passwords for all the sites she had accounts with—which, these programs are about the worst thing ever, by the way—trusting all your user names and passwords for everything, including banking, to a third party just isn't smart. Aside from that, the program does have account information for Classified OD saved in its memory. Though when I tried to access her account there, it told me that it was not a recognized user name and password. So I thought maybe she changed her password and filled out the 'lost my login' information form on the site, hoping that the site would send the reset information to her e-mail, which we have access to. We never got anything, meaning she must have closed her account there or had it closed by the company."

"Why would she have it closed by the company?" I asked.

"Ah, well when people post fake classified listings and get reported, the place could close the account."

I nodded. "Any signs that's what happened?"

O'Neil shook his head.

"Okay, so she did have an account at one time but no longer does. Can we see when it was closed?"

"I checked through her e-mail for one of the standard 'sorry to see you go' e-mails or anything from Classified OD, actually. Not a single message. Maybe the company keeps records of account terminations."

"Okay." I pulled my notepad out and jotted down what he'd said. "What's up with the tablet?"

"Dead as a doornail."

"Dead how?" I asked.

"Cooked from the inside, just like the cell phone I was looking into."

"You can't get anything from it?"

"No, but I think I know how it was fried."

"How's that?"

"Well, I'm thinking that someone sent the tablet, cell phone, and computer a virus," he said.

"The cell phone. This is Jasmine Thomas's as well?" I asked. "If memory serves, it was the only one found."

Skip cleared his throat and responded. "That was the name on it, yeah."

O'Neil continued. "Well, the reason I think that someone sent it is this." He turned and clicked a few buttons on his computer. A window popped up on his monitor with what looked like some kind of computer code on it.

"What am I looking at?" I asked.

"A virus, worm, bug, whatever you want to call it," O'Neil said. "I found this running in the background on the computer. It's odd, not a normal computer virus."

"What's it do?"

"Well, as far as I can tell, it's designed to be a virus for a cell phone. The commands look like the virus erases a bunch of information and then it gets into the power settings—my guess would be to overload the main board and memory—essentially frying the phone. Apparently, it works on tablets as well. I opened the tablet up, and the damage looks consistent with the damage inside of the cell phone we have."

"Okay, so how do we find out where it came from or who sent it?" I asked.

"Well, that's significantly more difficult. If it's targeted to phones, I'd have to think it would be an attachment to an e-mail or a text message. I guess it could have also came from an app or something else downloaded to the device."

"So we've found something that we can't do anything with?"

"I'm still looking into it," O'Neil said. "I'm going to go through every piece of code on the virus that I can and see if maybe I can see exactly what it is targeting or how it is being installed on the devices. That, and I'm going to make some calls to see if anyone else may have some insight into it."

I nodded. "Okay." I looked at Agent Toms and Skip. "You guys just want to let me know if there's a development with this?"

"Sure," Toms said.

I looked back at O'Neil. "There's no way you can get the tablet back up and running?"

"Even if I did, the memory is cooked. It's a paperweight," he said.

"Do what you can with the virus and computer. I should be bringing you another computer tomorrow. I have a meeting set up with a family member, and she's going to give us her daughter's, a victim's, laptop."

"Sure. I'll be watching for it."

"Thanks," I said.

My cell phone buzzed in my pocket. I pulled it out and looked at the screen, which showed a text message from Beth, saying: *Back at the FBI building.*

I looked at Agent Toms and Skip. "Should be all I need, I guess. My partner is back in the building. I need to find her and get going on getting a subpoena ready."

"I'll walk with you back over there," Agent Toms said.

"Skip, let me give you my direct number in case you get something and I'm out chasing around," I said.

"Sure," he said.

I wrote my number down on my notepad and tore off the page for him.

CHAPTER TWENTY-SEVEN

Brett sat at his desk in a fog. He had a meeting in twenty minutes with a couple representatives of a local charity looking to finalize a donation. He needed sleep.

Brett thumbed the button on his desk phone to ring Carrie.

"Need something, sir?" she asked over the speaker phone.

"A coffee. And cancel everything after these charity people. I'm not feeling well and am going to head home."

"Okay, did you want me to reschedule the appointments from this afternoon to next week?"

"Whenever you can fit them in is fine."

"Okay, you said no calls, but Tom has called up from legal twice. It sounded important."

"What did he want?"

"He didn't say. But like I said, he's called up here twice looking for you in the last twenty minutes or so."

"Okay, I'll call down to him. Thanks, Carrie."

"Sure, I'll have your coffee in a minute," she said.

Brett clicked off, picked up the phone's receiver, and

rested it on his shoulder. He called the legal department.

"Legal," a woman answered.

"Hi, it's Mr. Bailor. I'm looking for Tom."

"One moment, sir."

The phone clicked and rang again in Brett's ear.

"Mr. Bailor?" a man asked.

"Yeah, Tom. What's going on?"

"Well, we have a federal agent here with a subpoena. Just wanted to let you know."

"Okay. What is the subpoena requesting?" Brett asked.

"Records for all communication through the site on a woman. Um, name is Rebecca Wright."

"Okay. Is everything being put together to satisfy the subpoena?"

"Yeah, I made a call to the development department, and they are putting it together as we speak."

"Sure. Just make sure the agent has everything he needs," Brett said.

"Yeah, okay. Um, one second, Mr. Bailor."

Brett could hear him speaking with someone in the background.

Tom came back on the phone. "Sorry about that. Michelle just came in. It looks like we have another two agents here now with another subpoena."

"For?" Brett asked.

"I haven't looked at it yet."

"I'll come down. See you in a second." Brett hung up and stood from his desk. As he walked toward his office door, he heard a knock, and the door opened.

Carrie, his secretary, stood in the doorway with his cup of coffee. She held it out toward him. "Mr. White and one of his colleagues are here."

Brett gave her a confused look as he took the coffee.

"From the charity, your twelve o'clock," Carrie said.

"Can you reschedule them? It sounds like there is something going on down in legal that needs my attention."

"They're sitting in the waiting area, sir," Carrie said.

He let out a puff of air and slid past her in the doorway. Brett walked to the waiting area, where the visitors had taken seats.

"I'm Brett Bailor," he said. "I just wanted to come and personally apologize. We're going to need to reschedule the meeting we had set for today. There's something urgent that requires my attention."

An older man with short white hair and a mustache sat with one leg on top of his other knee. A portfolio folder rested on his lap. "Oh, um, well we needed to get this taken care of before the fundraiser this weekend," Mr. White said.

"Again, I apologize. Maybe my secretary can reschedule something for tomorrow."

Brett stared at the man and the woman beside him, hoping they would accept the rescheduling and leave.

The woman stood. She appeared to be in her sixties and annoyed. She had short blond—obviously dyed—hair and wore a tan pantsuit. "We drove three hours. This should only take a minute." Her tone of voice had a ring of authority, as if she was used to getting her way.

"Sorry. Again, I apologize," Brett said.

"Mostly, we just need your signature on this pledge," she said. "I guess we could work out the rest by phone." She tried handing Brett the portfolio that she'd taken from Mr. White. She flipped the cover open and pointed to where he should sign.

"I'd want to look over the paperwork. I just don't have time at the moment," he said.

"For a signature?" she asked. "Are you serious? You've already seen the paperwork."

Brett clenched his jaw. The woman was trying to strongarm him. That was something he wouldn't stand for—not in his place of business. He tried to remain professional though his mind was envisioning beating her to death where she stood.

Brett cracked his neck from side to side. "Ma'am, what came up requires my immediate attention. I'd like to reschedule. If we can't, I guess we'll just have to decline. Now, you can see Carrie for an appointment if you'd like, but I must be going."

He left for the elevator—he had more important things to worry about at that moment. Brett rounded the corner and thumbed the elevator button to take him downstairs. He boarded the elevator and stepped out on the forty-sixth floor—legal. He walked down the hall and entered the office.

Brett noticed people he assumed to be the federal agents, two men and a woman, sitting in the waiting area. He continued past to Tom's office, rapped his knuckles on the door, and entered.

"Are those the feds in the waiting room?" he asked.

"Hard to miss," Tom said.

"And the second subpoena?" Brett asked.

"It's for the same thing but on a different woman. A Jasmine Thomas."

Brett nodded.

"One of the feds that just showed asked if he could

speak with someone in the website-development department as well. I figured I'd let you field that."

"Sure. Get together everything they've requested. I'll go and speak with them regarding the site."

"Okay. These names on the subpoenas—they are homicide victims. I recognize the one name from the news coverage," Tom said.

Brett put on his best look of confusion. "I haven't been watching local coverage in a bit."

"Yeah, big news. Serial killer."

"Serial killer, huh? Well, let's get these agents everything they need."

"Sure. The guys should have all the transcripts for them shortly."

Brett nodded and left the office. He walked to the waiting room and stood before the seated agents, quickly taking them in. The two men wore suits and looked the part of federal agents, and the woman who sat between them was dressed for business and attractive. Brett clasped his hands behind his back. "I'm Brett Bailor, founder of Classified OD. My guys are working on getting everything you requested now. It should just be a bit. I was informed that one of you had a couple of questions regarding website development?"

The fed seated on the left stood. He appeared a few inches over six foot and wore a black suit with a white dress shirt and a navy-blue tie. His hair was short and dark, and his face had a bit of black-and-gray stubble.

"Agent Hank Rawlings," the man said. "These are Agents Harper and Andrews. I did have a few questions regarding how profiles for your users are handled."

"Sure, I should be able to answer those questions for

you," Brett said. "I'm also the lead website engineer."

"Founder and engineer?" the other male fed asked.

Brett nodded. "I built the site and the company from the ground up. I don't want someone else tinkering with my pride and joy." Brett looked at the agents, but none of them responded. His eyes came to rest on the brunette female agent. "Why don't you guys come with me to the conference lounge down the hall—a little more comfortable. I'll have someone from legal bring everything to us as soon as it's set. It will be a little more private to talk as well if you have some questions."

Agent Rawlings nodded and motioned for Brett to lead the way, so he did. Brett walked the group down the hall and into a large office filled with executive chairs surrounding a circular table. After sitting the agents down, he asked, "Water, coffee, soda? I can have whatever you'd like brought."

All three agents declined.

"Did you speak with another agent on the telephone the other day?" asked the fed named Rawlings.

Brett gave Agent Rawlings his attention. "I did. The agent I spoke with the other day, he didn't really give me the specifics of what information he was requesting." He paused. "The man who heads up the legal office said that he recognized the names on the subpoenas as two murder victims that have been all over the news. Was this the information that the other agent was referring to?"

"It was," Agent Rawlings said.

"I wish I would have known that. Forget subpoenas and the legal department. I sure as hell won't let my website be a place to facilitate things of that nature. What can I do to help?"

"Release all the documents you may have for each victim," the woman agent said.

"Absolutely. That goes without question, whatever you need. Do you know for certain that they were all users?"

"We have a good idea that they were," she said.

"Sure. Why don't you give me the names, and I'll have someone get you everything you need. As far as the profiles, what were your questions there?" Brett looked at the agent named Rawlings and waited for a response.

CHAPTER TWENTY-EIGHT

Andrews, Beth, and I entered a small conference room back at the Chicago FBI office. Mr. Bailor, at Classified OD, had searched each woman's name for us and provided us with everything they had. He informed us that once users deleted their profiles, they were gone for good. Aside from holding past users personal information becoming a privacy-related issue, he explained that the company simply couldn't retain every user's information after they quit using the site—doing so would take up too much space on their servers, costing the company excess money. We wouldn't be able to get anything on Jasmine Thomas even though we had evidence on her computer that she had had an account, at one time, on the site. Mr. Bailor also let us know that the company didn't keep records of account termination dates.

We took seats around the table, where Andrews dropped the file box Mr. Bailor had given us. He opened the top and pulled the smaller files from within.

"So we just got Monica Whickham, our latest victim, and Rebecca Wright?" I asked.

"That's it," Andrews said. "Nothing on the others, unfortunately. Looks like there are a fair number of transcripts in here, though."

"Well, let's dig in. See if we can find a smoking gun somewhere," Beth said.

"How do we want to do it?" Andrews asked.

"Write down all the user names Monica and Rebecca were in contact with. If we find a match between the two, well, that's our lead," I said.

"Are we just digging through these and trying to find messages that are from the personals section?" Andrews asked. "It looks like each of these pages have what segment of the website they came from listed at the top."

I motioned for him to hand me some of the transcripts. "Everything. Personals and everything else."

"Sure," Andrews said. He divvied up the transcripts, handing Beth and me each a stack and then taking a pile for himself.

I looked down at the sheets of paper—they belonged to Monica Whickham.

Beth leaned over, tucked her brown hair behind her ear, and looked to see which woman I was working on. "I have her too."

"Have who?" Andrews asked.

"Monica Whickham," Beth said.

"Oh. Yeah, looks like it's about fifty-fifty on transcripts between the two women. I have transcripts from her as well," he said. "We'll get her done and then move on to Rebecca Wright."

Beth nodded but said nothing.

My eyes went back to the sheet in front of me. The date on the top corner of the first message was from two weeks prior. The information on the page was oriented with outgoing messages on the left and incoming messages on the right. I pulled out my notepad and jotted down the user name of the person she was exchanging messages with—the conversation topic was an inquiry about a sale of a vehicle, which matched with the segment of the site that the message had come through. She appeared to be looking to buy a used car, due to the fact that the next few pages of messages were of a similar topic—her inquiring about the vehicles and trying to arrange times she'd be able to view them. The responses included a few addresses and first names. I wrote them down.

"Anything from the personals?" Beth asked.

I scratched the side of my cheek, feeling stubble that needed to be shaved. "Not yet. Looks like she was trying to buy a car, from what I'm seeing here."

"And rent a new apartment," Beth said. "These sheets look like they're all from the website's housing and for-rent section."

"I have some back and forths here that are from the personals section of the site," said Andrews. "I have three different users that she was corresponding with. A Mike Money Twelve; a Writeguy, with a *W* for write; and a Lady Killer Seventy-five."

Beth and I both looked up at Agent Andrews.

"Lady Killer?" I asked.

"Yeah," he said. "Think it's that obvious?"

"It would be pretty bad if it was. Keep looking," I said.

"Sure. I'm writing the handles down. The Classified OD owner gave us a profile sheet for each person included in each correspondence. The real names for these guys should be in there," Andrews said.

I went back to my stack of papers and continued writing down user names. We finished with Monica Whickham's transcripts in about an hour. The bottom of my pile of papers had some messages back and forth that had come through the personals section. The LadyKiller75 handle was the only person she had been speaking with in my stack of transcripts. Apparently, they were getting to know each other. The man asked about her family, brothers and sisters, where she worked, religion, and things of that nature, and she asked him about similar topics.

Nothing from Beth's pile of transcripts had anything other than Monica searching for an apartment or trying to buy miscellaneous items—she apparently had used the website to buy everything from shoes to furniture. Between Andrews, Beth, and I, we created one long master list of every user name she had contact with. Then we moved Monica's files off to one side and began on Rebecca Wright.

Andrews again went through the process of splitting up the transcripts and handing them out.

I took my stack of papers and glanced at the first sheet—the messages had come from the personals segment. I flipped through the first couple of pages, looking to see if any of the names matched up with the three we had on Monica—they didn't.

Before I flipped to the fourth page, Beth piped up. "Lady Killer Seventy-five." She slammed her finger down to the name on the page. "Both women spoke to him."

I leaned back in my office chair and ran my fingers through my hair. I nodded to Andrews. "Dig up the guy's profile sheet before we get any further into this."

Andrews dug through the file box and brought out a separate file. He began flipping through the papers, which I assumed to be the profile sheets. The stack of papers looked about an inch thick. Beth and I waited, watching him as he flipped from one page to the next.

He stopped and yanked a paper out. "Got it."

"What's his name?" I asked.

Andrews set the paper down on the desk before him. He ran his finger down the page and then spun it so it faced Beth and me.

"The guy's name is Jeff Mercer," Andrews said.

"Give an address?" Beth asked.

"No, let me go run the name and pull his information. I'll be right back." Andrews took the sheet and left the conference room.

I grabbed my notepad sitting next to me on the table and began flipping through pages.

"What are you looking for?" Beth asked.

"I'd written some names down. Hold on." I flipped through my notepad until I found my notes from the interviews with Jasmine Thomas's mother and my notes from the interview with the family of Kennedy Taylor. I found the page and ran my finger down the notes. "Here we go." I stared at what I'd written and shook my head.

"What?"

"Jasmine Thomas's mother mentioned the names Tom and Mark. Cassidy Taylor mentioned the name Rick as far as potential suitors."

"None of which are Jeff," Beth said. "But then again, we have no proof that this Jeff Mercer ever was in contact with the other women other than Monica and Rebecca."

I nodded. "Would have been nice to have a Jeff written

down." I started through the transcripts in front of me, looking for a message from the LadyKiller75 handle. I didn't find one. "Is he signing his name to those messages?" I asked.

"Um." She looked over the sheet in front of her. "Yeah. It says Jeff."

"Look and see if it does in the messages to Monica," I said.

Beth reached across the table and picked up Monica's file, which we'd set aside. She thumbed through the papers until she found one containing messages from our guy. "Says Jeff again."

"Okay."

"Think he was using different names or something?" she asked.

I shrugged. "Could have been."

The door of the room opened a moment later. "We have four by that name in the area," Andrews said. He slapped a sheet of paper against his hand. His mouth turned up into a smile. "But one of them lives in Aurora."

"Really?" I asked.

He nodded. "I passed Agent Toms on my way back in. He told me Agent Bower was still in the area. I called him up and told him to grab whoever was still out there and go try to pick this guy up. I guess this Mercer works at a tire shop in that area. So if he's not at home, maybe we can catch up with him at his work."

"Where would he be brought? Back here?" Beth asked.

"Yeah. We have interview rooms downstairs. Bower is going to call me back as soon as they locate the guy," Andrews said.

"Perfect," I said. "Let's get into all of his messages

with the victims and see what we can pull out. Look for anything mentioning meeting up, asking where they live, things like that. We need to find out if we can put these two with this guy around the time they went missing. It will give us some ammunition if we get him in here."

"Yeah, absolutely," Andrews said. He slid out his chair and took a seat.

We dug back into the transcripts from the messaging.

CHAPTER TWENTY-NINE

Andrews got the call just before we finished up going through the messages back and forth between the victims and Jeff Mercer. Bower and another agent had picked the guy up from his work and would be back at the FBI office any minute. The dump site for Monica's body and Rebecca's car was between the guy's home and the automotive shop where he was employed. However, looking at the correspondences between Monica, Rebecca and Mercer, the content of the messages didn't look as though either woman had ever personally met with the man. We did see phone numbers exchanged with Monica, yet we still didn't have her cell-phone records from her carrier to see if they had actually been in contact. We cross-referenced the number he'd given Monica with all of the other victims' phone records that the bureau already had—we didn't find a match.

Andrews and I sat in the observation room next to the interview room where Bower would lead Mercer when they arrived. The observation room door opened, and Beth walked in.

"What did Ball say?" I asked.

"Not much. He was in a meeting and could only talk for a second. I told him we had a potential that we were about to interview. Basically, he said keep doing what we're doing and he'd call after his meeting for a full update."

I nodded.

Beth took a seat next to Andrews and me.

"How are we playing this?" Andrews asked.

I looked at him. "Agent Bower didn't mention that this guy looked like he was in a scuffle at all, did he?"

Andrews shook his head. "Nope."

"Okay. Well, that's the first thing we should look for: bruising around knuckles, scratch marks or cuts on hands and arms. Chances are whoever did what they did to the third-shift worker—"

"Ted Biller," Andrews said.

"Chances are whoever put the beating on Ted Biller is showing signs that they were in a fight," I said.

"And if we get nothing there," Beth said, "we have to question him regarding all his correspondences with the two women."

"Right," I said. "Plus, we have the last-seen-and-spoken-with dates. Find out what he was doing on those dates. Finish up with why a woman's body he was in talks with, along with another deceased woman's car, also who he was in talks with, wound up in his town between his home and workplace."

"That's the question that will have him lawyering up," Andrews said.

"Which is why we save it for last. Let's get what we can out of him and save that," I said.

"So who's going in to question him?" Andrews asked. "All of us, one of us, two of us?"

"The guy's handle is lady killer," Beth said. "Let's see if he wants to talk to a lady."

I smirked. "I'm fine with that."

Andrews shrugged.

"If I can't get anywhere with him, I'll come out, and you two can go in together."

"Sure," Andrews said. "It looks like you're going to be on, here." He pointed through the observing glass. A man in a suit, who I assumed to be Agent Bower, was seating a man in the room.

Beth walked directly to the glass and stared in at him.

The man sitting looked to be in his early thirties. He was an inch or two under six foot and in average shape. He wore a dirty red shop shirt from the tire store he worked at, with a pair of black pants. The man had short dark hair and what looked like a small tattoo on the side of his neck. Both of his arms also had other various tattoos. I tried to get a look at his knuckles and paid close attention to his forearms, but I didn't spot any abrasions or signs that he'd been in a fight. However, something wasn't right with him. I thought back to the glimpse I'd seen of the man at the coffee shop.

"Does that look like the kind of guy who'd show up at a coffee shop in a suit and tie?" I asked.

Beth turned back from the glass and looked at me. "I don't think this guy has ever put on a suit in his life. Either way, he had contact with both women."

"True," I said.

Beth looked at Andrews. "The room is being recorded, correct?"

"Yeah," he said.

The door of the observation room opened, and the agent who had seated Mercer entered.

"Agents Rawlings and Harper, this is Agent Geoff Bower," Andrews said.

He shook my hand.

"Rawlings," I said.

He shook Beth's hand next and had a seat.

"Well, let's see what this guy has to say," Beth said. She walked to the door and exited.

"Did the guy give you any problems?" Andrews asked.

Agent Bower shook his head. "He seemed more scared than anything. I told him we'd like to ask him some questions regarding an investigation, and he came along quietly. He never even asked why. Never asked how he was supposed to get home. Nothing."

"Interesting," Andrews said. "Probably guilty of something."

Beth entered the room and took a seat across from the man, her back to us.

I glanced over at Andrews, who was fishing his cell phone from his pocket.

He stared down at the screen and then looked at me. "Press conference tomorrow morning at nine," he said.

I nodded. Then my attention went back to Beth inside the interview room.

She arranged her folder and cleared her throat. "I'm Agent Beth Harper. You're Mr. Jeff Mercer, correct?"

He nodded.

"Can you please give me a verbal answer? The room is being recorded, and we need audio as well as video," she said.

"Yes. Jeff Mercer," he said.

"First, do you know why we asked you in today?"

"I don't know."

"Well, if you had to guess," Beth said.

I watched as he squirmed in his chair. "Shit. I don't know. Because of what I've been doing online."

I looked over at Andrews, who leaned forward in his chair, staring through the glass into the observation room.

"And what is that exactly?" Beth asked.

Mercer didn't respond.

"Mr. Mercer?" Beth asked.

"Look, it wasn't even that much money. A ton of people do it. A couple hundred bucks, maybe a thousand at the most," he said. "I mean, is it that serious that the FBI wants to talk to me? Should I have a lawyer? Who said something? That Debbie chick?"

Beth cleared her throat. "No. Not Debbie. I have to say that it sounds like you're confessing to something."

"I'm not confessing to anything. I don't even think it's illegal."

"What exactly is it?" Beth asked.

"Just some whatever, talking to people, asking for help."

"I don't follow, Mr. Mercer. You're going to need to explain to me precisely what you're talking about."

He jerked his head back. "Well, if you don't know, I'm sure as hell not going to tell you and incriminate myself."

"Right," Beth said. "Why don't we just circle back around to that in a second?"

Mercer didn't respond.

Beth opened the file she'd taken in with her. She slipped out a few pieces of paper. "I'd like to show you a few things and then get your response."

"Yeah, whatever," he said.

"These are some transcripts of messages you had sent and received with a Monica Whickham." Beth slid one of the papers over to him. "This is you, correct?"

"Yeah, that's me," he said. "So what?"

"We'll get to the 'so what' part in a minute." Beth took the sheet away from him and pulled out another. "Now, this is the same thing between you and a Rebecca Wright."

"Okay," he said. "I talk to a lot of girls online. It's what I do."

"It's what you do?" Beth asked.

Mercer let out a grumble and adjusted himself in his chair. "Fine," he said. Mercer let out a huge breath. "I try to get money out of women I meet online."

Beth folded her arms on the table in front of her. "Expand on that."

"I contact just about every woman in the personals section. I try to build friendships with them, but it often turns into more, just online. I never meet up with them in person. I make excuses why I can't see them when they ask to meet up. It's usually a money-related excuse. The women that offer to help out with money, well, I take it and make up more excuses for more money."

"Right," Beth said. "So you were trying to scam these two women is what you're saying?"

"I don't know if I'd call it that, but…"

"No. I'm pretty sure scam is the right word for it," Beth said. "So you claim that you've never met either of these two women in person?"

Mercer shook his head. "Never. You should be able to see in those messages that we never got to the point of asking each other to meet up. Even if they asked, well, then I would have run my pitch about money."

Beth wrote something down. "Can I ask what you were doing last night?"

"Um, working until sixish, stopped at home for about an hour, and then went to a concert. I was at the concert until about midnight, and then I went out to a couple of bars with some friends until bar close."

"And these friends, what are their names?"

"Ugh, are you really going to call people and check?" Mercer asked.

"You better believe it," she said.

Mercer's shoulders sank. He rattled off a bunch of names then pulled out his phone and gave Beth a handful of phone numbers.

"Here, look." Mercer passed his phone to her. "Scroll to the right. Photos from the concert last night and a couple from the bar after."

Beth briefly looked at the phone and slid it back across the table to him.

"Okay," Beth said. "And after bar close, you did what exactly?"

Mercer put his phone back into his pocket. "Got dropped off at my house and passed out."

"Anyone who can verify all of that?" Beth asked.

"Sure. Everyone I went out with and my wife when I got home."

"Your wife?" Beth asked.

Mercer nodded. "Yeah. She was pissed. Waited up for me so she could read me the riot act for coming in late, drunk."

"Does she know about your online ventures?"

"No. And I'd prefer if it stayed that way. I don't cheat on her. I never meet the women I contact, ever."

"Right," Beth said. "Give me a minute, and I'll be back with you."

"Yeah, okay," Mercer said.

Beth stood from her chair, grabbed her notes, and left the room.

The door for the observation room opened a moment later. Beth walked in, closed the door, and leaned back into it. "Well?"

"What were the pictures he showed you?" I asked.

"They were posted on a social media site—him and some other people with a stage and band in the background. The date was last night," Beth said.

"Okay. The friends' names and numbers?"

Beth tore the page of notes from her notepad and handed it to me.

"I'm going to get back in touch with the owner of Classified OD and get all this guy's transcripts. We'll see if in fact he's running his woman-scam deal," Andrews said.

"What do your guts say? Our guy or no?" Beth asked.

"I don't think so. Let me call these people quick to verify that he was with them," I said.

"Okay," Beth said. "I'm going to head back in and get his whereabouts on the other dates, as well as what concert he was at last night. He's a talker. I'll keep him talking while you guys check some things out."

"Sounds good." Andrews picked up the phone in the room to call Classified OD.

I rocked back in my chair but said nothing. I slid out my cell phone and dialed the first number on the sheet.

CHAPTER THIRTY

Brett's cell phone vibrated and buzzed across the nightstand next to his bed. He cracked his eyes open, let out a grunt of frustration, and reached for it. The number on the screen showed the call was coming from the legal office. Brett scooted himself up against his headboard, to a sitting position, and clicked Talk.

"Brett Bailor," he said.

"It's Tom. One of the feds that was in here earlier is calling back. He's looking for you. I told him you were out of the office for the rest of the day."

"What did he want?"

"He didn't say. He called the office here, and Brittany up front sent the call back to me. He basically just asked for you."

"Did he give you a callback number?" Brett asked.

"Yeah, he did. Did you want it?"

"Sure. Hold on." Brett slid open the drawer on his nightstand and pulled out a pen and paper. "Okay, what is it?"

Tom gave him the number.

"I'll give the guy a call back and see what he wanted. Which agent was it?" Brett asked.

"Agent Andrews."

"Okay. Thanks, Tom."

Brett hung up, rubbed his eyes, and rolled out of bed. In the bathroom, he splashed some water over his face, and then he headed down the hallway to his home office. After taking a seat in front of the computer, he woke it up by wiggling the mouse. He caught the time in the bottom right-hand corner of his desktop: 4:08 p.m.

The hour-and-a-half nap he'd had would have to do for the time being.

Brett dialed the fed back and cleared his throat as the phone rang in his ear.

"Agent Andrews," a man answered.

"Hi, Brett Bailor calling back," he said.

"Hello, Mr. Bailor. We were wondering if you could give us a hand with a bit more information."

"Absolutely, if I can. Though I won't be back in the office until tomorrow."

"Well, let me tell you what we need, and we'll take it from there," the agent said.

"Sure."

"We went through the women's transcripts you'd sent us off with and found a common user that both women were speaking with."

"Okay, that's a good thing, right? I mean, as far as your investigation goes," Brett said.

"Well, we're getting somewhere, so that's something. The thing is, we have the man in for questioning as we speak and we're trying to check out his alibi. We'd like his transcripts to see who else this man was in contact with and the nature of the conversations."

Brett was quiet for a moment. He knew as soon as he gave the FBI Mercer's transcripts, he'd be cleared. Brett began to second-guess his idea of giving the feds a suspect in the first place.

"Ugh," Brett said. "Well, I'd have to be there to get them for you. I don't have access to the system at the moment, and in order to get them from the system files, they would need to have administrative access, which only I and my development manager have. The problem is he's on vacation. Tell you what, I'll be back in the office tomorrow morning, I can get it put together and either faxed over to you or e-mailed as soon as I get in. Will that work?"

The agent let out a breath. "Um, if that's the soonest we could get it."

"Yeah, unfortunately, it's going to be. I'm on duty for my son's soccer game. That means hauling the whole gang around, pizza after, the works. Do you have children?" Brett asked.

"I do. Two daughters. I know how it goes. That's fine. As soon as you can get it to us in the morning, that would be fine."

"Sure. I'll call this number and get the information as far as where to send it in the morning."

"I appreciate it, Mr. Bailor," the agent said.

"Yup, no problem," Brett said. "We'll talk in the morning. Have a good evening."

Brett hung up and dropped his phone onto his desk. "Shit." Brett scratched at his hairline in the front, trying to think of what to do. He debated going into the system files and creating messages to seal Mercer's fate—it was an option. However, that would give the feds further cause to look into his company—something Brett had no interest in, for there was always a chance they could find something if their tech guys started sniffing around. Aside from that, Classified OD would be dragged through the mud in the press, giving the company a bad image, which meant angry shareholders. In the morning, Brett would give them what the agent had requested and hope that would be the end of it.

Brett grabbed his phone and headed back for the bedroom. He heard a phone ringing as he walked down the hallway—not the one that he was holding. Brett stopped and realized the ringing was coming from behind him, back in the office.

"Prepaid," he said. "Hmm."

Brett turned and headed back the way he'd come. He took a seat back in his office chair and opened the rolling drawer to the side. He reached inside and scooped up the phone—the number was from the area, but not one he recognized. He let the call go to the automated voice mail and stared at the screen, waiting to see if the caller left a message. A moment later, the voice-mail icon lit up in the top left of the screen, so he hit the button to check the message.

Hey it's Mandy. I hope I have the right number. I wanted to see if maybe you were interested in lunch tomorrow. Give me a call back and let me know. No worries if you're busy. We could maybe try another day or something. Hope you're doing well. See ya.

Brett smiled widely and hit the button to erase the message. He pulled up the call log on his phone and hit the button to call her back. The phone rang in his ear.

CHAPTER THIRTY-ONE

Beth and I got back to the hotel around seven o'clock. Andrews had said he couldn't get the transcripts from Classified OD until the morning, so we'd be waiting on that. I spoke with each of Mercer's friends, and then his wife. His alibi checked out with everyone. His wife seemed to be well aware of his online activities but never brought it up to her husband.

Beth got his whereabouts for the times the other women had last been seen and found. The main thing saving him was that he raced dirt bikes on the weekends, sometimes taking Fridays off and leaving Thursday nights. He'd provided proof of events attended and locations that put him out of the area when two of the women were last seen and their bodies found. The logistics of him having committed the crimes and traveling for his racing just didn't line up. We still planned to go through the transcripts when they showed up, but Mercer wasn't looking like our guy. They kicked him loose from questioning a bit after six.

Beth sat in my room on the wingback chair, one leg

resting on her other knee. She was jotting down notes in her notepad. "What time were you meeting with Angela Wormack's mother tomorrow?"

I turned in my desk chair and faced her. "Ten." I rolled my head to the side. "Shit."

"Shit what?" Beth asked.

I let out a breath. "Andrews wanted to do that press conference at nine. Son of a bitch."

"I'll handle meeting with her if you need to be with Andrews at the press conference."

"Are you sure?"

"Yeah, that's fine. Where does she live?"

"Hold on. I'll get you the address." I spun back in my chair and found it in my file then walked it over and handed it to Beth.

She took the piece of paper and found the address. "Oh, okay, Bolingbrook. That's about an hour from here. No problem."

"You're sure you don't mind?" I asked.

"Anything that keeps me away from speaking under pressure, I'm fine with."

"All right."

"So she's giving us a computer?" Beth asked.

"She said she would, yes. The mother's name is Hilary. Same last name, Wormack. I'll send you with my notes from the phone call I had with her as well, so you can see what we talked about and see if there's anything you want to follow up on." I walked back to the desk, grabbed my notepad, and flipped through the pages until I found the notes from the phone call. I ripped the two pages out and walked them back to Beth.

She slipped the papers into a folder and closed the top

as I went back to my desk.

"What the tech guys found is bugging me," Beth said.

"How's that?"

"Well, from what you described when we were driving over to the Classified OD office, the virus could kill cell phones and tablets and erase histories."

"That's what the tech guys said, yeah," I said.

"And there was also login information from Jasmine for Classified OD on her computer, but the credentials no longer worked."

"Right," I said.

"Well, who is to say that the virus—or person behind the virus—couldn't have deleted their accounts at Classified OD?"

"Fair question."

"You said the tech guys at the Chicago office had the virus?"

"Um." I scratched my cheek. "I mean, I guess that's what I was looking at. The tech guy—ah, what the hell was his name—O'Neil, showed me something on a screen that was just numbers and symbols and commands, computer gibberish. He said it was the virus."

"Okay. I'm wondering if there is a way he can send that to the twins back in Virginia and see if they can come up with anything on it," Beth said.

"Probably worth a shot if it's possible. The guy running the tech unit there was named Skip."

"Okay, I'm going to head back to my room and call there and then call back to Virginia. Speaking of which, Ball wanted you to call him."

"Sure," I said.

"Okay, I'll be back over here in an hour or so. We're

going to go get a drink. No excuses, no bullshit, and no talk about the investigation."

I flashed her a smile. "We'll see," I said.

Beth nodded. "That's pretty close to a yes." She grabbed her paperwork and left my room.

I picked up my phone and dialed Ball. He answered in two rings.

"Ball," he said.

"Hey, it's Hank. Beth said you wanted me to call."

"Yeah. How's it going out there?"

"Oh, I thought Beth gave you an update a little bit ago."

"She did. I want to hear it from you," Ball said.

"Well, we've been running pretty much nonstop. We thought we had a suspect, but it's looking like that fizzled out. We have some leads, but actual evidence seems a little hard to come by."

"When you look at the investigation as a whole, what is sticking out at you?" Ball asked.

"Classified OD and whoever is doing this has some form of a personal relationship with the victims. We got the transcripts from the place for the two latest victims, but it didn't show them corresponding with anyone in common other than the guy we questioned—that was the suspect that fizzled out."

"We should look into every correspondence and the people behind them, not just what matches on the surface. This guy could be using different handles, different IP addresses, things like that. You can send the transcripts back here, and I'll have Marcus and Lewis get on it."

"Sure. I'll have Andrews get them back to you guys," I said.

"Okay. What else?" he asked. "The tech stuff."

"A computer with a virus that looked like it was capable of frying cell phones and tablets. Beth was actually going to see if the virus itself could be sent to the Phillips guys in our tech department so they could have a look at it."

"Okay. What do you have tomorrow?"

"Beth is meeting with the mother of our first victim tomorrow morning at ten while I run a press conference with the local bureau. The mother Beth is meeting with is going to give us another computer to check out. After that, I don't know."

Ball cleared his throat. "See what you get tomorrow and Saturday. If nothing looks promising, we'll bring you guys back Sunday. You guys can work on it here and coordinate with the Chicago office if needed."

"That's fine."

"How's working with Beth?"

The question caught me a little off guard. "Fine. No problems that I can think of," I said. I didn't really know what kind of response he was looking for.

"Good. She says you're giving it a hundred percent plus. Keep up the good work. We'll talk tomorrow."

"Okay, we'll see you," I said and hung up.

His "keep up the good work" comment frustrated me. I didn't feel as though I was getting anywhere, two bodies had been found since we'd been on the investigation, and we still didn't have a sniff of a suspect—that didn't qualify as "good work" in my book.

I let out a breath and dialed Karen.

"Hey," Karen said. "Remember me?"

"Sorry, I've been busier than hell. Dead bodies,

driving, interviewing, questioning, checking. Yet here I am at the end of the day with squat to show for it."

"If this guy was easy to catch, he would have already been caught," Karen said.

I didn't respond.

"You know I'm right. Say it."

"You're right, dear," I said. "How's home?"

"Okay. I miss you, though. Any idea how long you're still going to be there?"

"Actually, yeah, I just got off the phone with Ball. He said he was bringing us back on Sunday."

"So what if you're still in the same situation as you are now?" she asked.

"Work the case from back in Virginia. Coordinate with Andrews here would be my guess."

"Andrews? I assume an agent there."

"Yeah, he's the agent that is running the investigation locally."

"Ah, got it," she said. "So what's the plan for the rest of your night?"

I rocked back in my chair. "I don't know. I need to call Andrews quick. After that, I'm not so sure. Beth wanted to go grab a drink. I might do that or just sit here in front of the television and talk to you."

"You might want to go have that drink," she said.

"Why is that?"

"Well, I think I'm actually going to be busy this evening." She worded the end of her sentence as though it was a question.

"Busy doing?"

"Poker. Sounds like we'll have enough for a full table."

"At our place?"

"Yeah, I got all the boxes put away and the place cleaned up," she said. "One of the guys is bringing over a table. We'll probably only play to midnight or so. That's okay, right? I know you don't like it when I have people over to play."

"No. That's not it. It's fine that you have people over to play cards. I just don't like cigar smoking in the house."

"I know, I know. One hundred percent—no one smokes inside."

"Then it's perfectly fine. I have to say though, I feel like our roles should be opposite in this conversation. Like I should be having the guys over to play poker and should be the one checking with you. You know what I mean? I think I'm going to start inviting a bunch of women over for scrapbooking parties."

"I want to see that." Karen laughed. "And let's think about this: aren't you in a hotel, states away, with a single, attractive woman?"

"Point taken," I said.

"Exactly. Anyway, do you want me to call you when everyone leaves?"

"Of course."

"Okay, I love you," Karen said.

"Love you, too. And make me some money."

"I will."

"Later, babe." I hung up and dialed Andrews.

CHAPTER THIRTY-TWO

The start of my morning had been a complete blur. I spoke with Beth briefly before I headed out, fought through traffic, talked to Ball, spilled some coffee on myself, and got to the Chicago FBI building. Beth was going to give me a call when she finished interviewing Hilary Wormack.

I'd met with Agent Andrews and Ted Springfield, the Chicago FBI office's PR manager, a bit before nine o'clock. We went over what would be included in the press release before delivering it to a packed and unruly media room. The reporters' questions were flying. All we could tell them was we were actively working the case and following up on every lead—it hadn't been enough for their liking.

I followed Andrews back up to and through the serial crimes unit and to his office. I took a seat in one of his guest chairs.

Andrews rounded his desk and sat down. He rocked back in his chair, unbuttoned the top button on his light-blue dress shirt and loosened his red patterned necktie. He clasped his hands behind his head and let out a deep breath. "Well, that went about how I thought it would."

I shrugged. "I mean, what can we really say other than we're following leads, doing everything we can. The press—and pretty much everyone else—don't want to hear anything other than we have someone in custody. Until those words get spoken, from the outside, it won't look like we're doing enough."

"I know," Andrews said. "I just wish we had more to give them. The public being scared is a bad thing."

I nodded. "Those profiles from the people that were in contact with Rebecca and Monica which you sent off got back to my home office. I spoke with my supervisor. My team back there is looking into them."

Andrews nodded and leaned forward in his chair. He hit a flashing red button on his desk telephone. Then he picked up the receiver, held it to his ear, and pressed a button on the phone's base.

I could hear the faint sound of a message playing in his ear.

Andrews clicked the button to hang up and then dialed a three-digit number—an internal call, probably. He looked at me. "We may have something here."

"Okay, what?"

He held his finger up at me to hold the question. "Yeah, Skip. What did you guys get?" Andrews asked.

I watched as Andrews nodded along as Skip, the lead in their tech unit, informed him of something.

"And you're certain?" Andrews asked. "A hundred percent? Okay. We'll talk in a bit." Andrews hung up. "The virus originated through the Classified OD messaging app."

"How do they know that's where it came from?"

"I didn't get into it with him."

"Okay. I'm sure it could be attached to a message or something. It's a bit more information, but we kind of already figured whoever was doing this was using the site."

"No. He said the message originated through the app itself," Andrews said. "It wasn't an attachment."

"Okay." I rubbed the back of my neck. "This place just keeps turning up. There's got to be a reason."

"Exactly. Speaking of which, I never got a call from Mr. Bailor this morning. He was supposed to send me over the transcripts from Mercer. He said he'd do it as soon as he got in. He also said he'd call me, which he hasn't."

A thought was bubbling in my head. "Well, wait. If it came through the messaging application for the website, why were there no transcripts on the other women? I find it a bit coincidental that three of five deceased women all canceled their accounts right before going missing."

"I have to agree with you there. Let me try calling Bailor and see what he says. Who knows, maybe he doesn't start until ten or something." Andrews picked up his desk phone and dialed. A moment later, he clicked off. "Voice mail. I'll try the Classified OD offices downtown." He dialed again. "Um, yes, this is Agent Andrews, looking for Brett Bailor."

He received some kind of response.

"Do you know when he'll be in today? I was waiting on him to send me some information over."

Andrews paused for a moment.

"He's not? Ah, okay. Thank you. No. No message." Andrews hung up.

"Not in?" I asked.

"No, and won't be back until Monday. I just talked to him last night. He specifically said he would send over the information first thing today. I even made a point to ask if it was the earliest I'd be able to get the transcripts." Andrews shook his head. "People piss me off."

"Big-shot owner of a company like that probably cares about two things—himself and his business. Sure, he'll put on the helpful face when there are FBI agents in front of him, but I doubt he actually gives two shits about our investigation," I said.

Andrews wore a look of annoyance and lifted his palms into the air. "The hell with it. I'm going to head over there and try to talk with someone else in the web-development department. Maybe they can answer some questions. Want to take a ride?"

"Sure. Let me call Beth quick and let her know we're heading over there." I glanced down at my watch—a couple minutes before ten o'clock. I pulled out my phone and dialed Beth's number.

She answered right away. "What's up? How did the press conference go?"

"The press conference was fine. Just wanted to let you know that Andrews and I are heading back over to the Classified OD offices downtown. Not sure when we'll be back at the field office."

"Oh, okay. Why the trip?"

"Skip, the lead in their tech department said that the virus came through the Classified OD messaging app, which raises a ton of questions. Andrews tried calling Bailor, the whatever you want to call him—owner, developer guy. Either way, he didn't answer, and he won't be back until Monday even though he was supposed to be in contact with Andrews this morning. Andrews and I are going to take a ride over there and see if we can get some answers from anyone else."

"Um, okay, you'll have to give me some more details on that later."

"I will."

"All right. I'm just getting to Bolingbrook now. Figure this may take me an hour or so, and then I'll head back. I'll give you a call when I leave, to see where you're at."

"Sure. Sounds good."

"Talk to you in a bit." Beth hung up.

I stuffed my phone back into my pocket and looked at Andrews. "I'm ready. She's going to call when she's finished out there."

Andrews stood and pulled his blue FBI jacket from the back of his office chair. He draped it over one shoulder and headed for the door. "Did you want to just ride with me over there?"

"Yeah, that's fine. I'm pretty much fed up with driving around here."

"It's not for the faint of heart."

I followed Andrews from the building and out to his car in the lot. We hopped in and headed for the Classified OD downtown office—a ten-minute ride. We parked in the same structure Beth and I had the day prior and then walked the block and a half to the fifty-story Madison Street high-rise containing the Classified OD offices. Andrews and I walked through the rotating door into the large lobby. The gray speckled marble floors reflected the light coming from overhead. We walked to the far right of the lobby, past a thirty-foot modern-art-looking sculpture, to a set of escalators. We rode up and found the listing of businesses and floors laid out on a big sign near the elevators. Classified OD took up floors forty-three to forty-eight of the building. "Web Div" was listed on floor forty-four.

"Guessing that's it," I said, pointing.

We checked the rest of the departments and didn't find anything that made us think otherwise.

Andrews and I walked to the nearest elevator, where a group of people waited to head up. The doors opened and took us all inside. Andrews thumbed the button for floor forty-four. The doors closed, and we began our trip up, stopping close to ten times to let people off and pick up new ones who also got off before our stop. By the time we reached floor forty-four, just Andrews, myself, and an older woman that looked somewhat familiar, remained. When I saw she was headed to floor forty-six, I knew why—she had been one of the women answering phones at the front desk of Classified OD's legal department.

We left the elevator and headed around the corner. A long hallway lined with office doors spread to our left and right. I caught a couple people walking the hall holding paperwork and files in their hands. We started down the hallway toward them, reading the individual doors as we went—the doors all said Web Div with an associated number behind it. We weren't going to get anywhere unless we had help.

I walked toward two women standing in the hall, chatting. Both looked to be in their later forties, and both wore business-casual clothing. I put them as some kind of administrative workers as I didn't see them doing any kind of IT work. They stopped their conversation abruptly and looked at me as I approached.

"Sorry, I'm looking for the web-development division," I said.

"You found it," said the woman on the left, leaning against the wall. "Who are you looking for, exactly?"

"Well, we're not sure. We have some questions for whoever can help us—basically, how the nuts and bolts of the website itself works."

The woman on the right told the other they would catch up later and asked me to follow her. I got Andrews's attention and waved him over.

"I'll let you talk to Ben Miglin. He handles support here. If anyone knows how something works around here, it's him or Mr. Bailor," she said.

"Thank you," I said.

She turned the corner and entered an office marked Web Div 4408. Andrews and I followed her inside. The office wasn't what I'd expected. Gray cubicles filled the center of the room, and a few offices with closed doors lined the sides. The carpet looked a bit dingy, and the room was windowless. She walked us past the cubicles to an office on the far right side near the back. Through the window in the door, I saw a man sitting inside at a computer.

The woman opened the door and stuck her head inside. She said something quiet to the man, and he asked her to send us in.

"You guys can go in," she said.

I nodded, passed her, and entered the man's office. Andrews followed me inside.

"What, um… What can I help you gentlemen with?" he asked.

"Agents Andrews and Rawlings with the FBI. We had some questions maybe you could help us out with," I said.

CHAPTER THIRTY-THREE

Brett gave his neck a small squirt of cologne and looked at himself in his bathroom mirror. He bared his flawless teeth at his reflection while he styled his hair. Brett was just about set—he had a lunch date with Mandy at one but needed to be out to her house by noon or so to pick her up. His cell phone rang on the bathroom counter. The office was calling him. He'd called Carrie and said he wouldn't be in and didn't want to be disturbed. Apparently, she couldn't follow directions. Brett clicked Talk.

"I said no calls," Brett answered.

"Um, Mr. Bailor?" a man asked.

"Yes."

"It's Tom from legal. Carrie just put me through to you."

"Yeah, Tom. What can I do for you?"

"Well, my secretary just popped in my office and said that two of those FBI agents that served us subpoenas were in the building again."

"Ah, dammit," Brett said. "I completely forgot. I was supposed to get some information for them put together and sent over this morning. Let me call the agent I spoke with. I appreciate you giving me the heads up."

"No problem," Tom said.

Brett hung up, found the number for the agent, and dialed. He walked from the master bathroom to his home office and took a seat behind his desk.

"Agent Andrews," a man answered.

"Hi. Brett Bailor. I have to apologize, I got everything set with my intern to call you and send you those documents this morning. I'm just finding out now that he didn't." That was a lie, but Brett figured it sounded believable enough.

"Okay, well, we're actually here now with…" The agent asked someone what their name was again. "With Ben Miglin."

"Oh, okay. Ben won't have access to what you requested, though. Let me get your e-mail, and I'll send you those transcripts personally."

The agent gave it to him.

Brett took a pen and paper from the desk and wrote it down. "You should see that shortly. Anything else?"

"Actually, yes. One moment."

Brett could hear him talking to someone but couldn't make out what was being said.

"Okay, sorry about that," the agent said. "We have some… I guess I don't know how else to describe it other than 'problems.'"

"Problems? Um, okay," Brett said.

"Yeah, it seems that there was a virus that had come through to these victims' electronic devices. The virus was distributed through your website's messaging app."

"Well, um… I mean, I guess that's possible. Probably

attached to a message or something."

"Our tech guys explained it to me that it originated from the app, meaning it wasn't included as an attachment."

"Oh, that's a bit more troubling," Brett said. "Yet if someone can hack into your e-mail and social-media accounts, I guess they could probably figure out a way to hack into our messaging system. This is the first I'm hearing about it, though. I'm going to have to get some of my guys on it."

"We're really leaning toward the idea that all of these victims were preyed upon through your website. It's really the only logical conclusion."

"Um, I'd hate to think that is the case, but if that is what happened... I mean, I don't know. However I can help you guys, I obviously will. I'm just not sure what I can do."

"It would really help us if there was a way to get deleted profiles and messages. Even a date of deletion would help," the agent said.

Brett let out a breath. "Yeah, like I said, we just don't store that information. I kind of wish we did now. I tell you what—let me make a couple of calls to other people in the industry and see if they have any ideas. Maybe someone smarter than me can say something that will spark the lightbulb over my head."

"I'd appreciate it," the agent said.

"I'll give you a call back in a bit."

"Thanks."

Brett hung up and tossed his phone onto the desk. He leaned back in his chair, shaking his head. He didn't need anyone from his web-development unit talking with feds.

They'd certainly tell the agents that old profiles were, in fact, retrievable. Brett picked his phone back up and dialed Tom in legal.

"Tom Mears."

"It's Brett. Those agents are now on the web-development floor doing who knows what. Find them and shoo them out of the building. Tell them to get warrants if they give you any issues."

"Um, okay," Tom said. "Can I ask why the sudden change of heart? I mean, it seemed like you wanted to go above and beyond, helping them yesterday."

"Of course. If I'm there, it's one thing. I'll do what I can. But I'm not going to let them just come in and take up my team's time with whatever they are doing, wandering around unattended and asking my staff questions."

"Completely understandable. Need a call back?" Tom asked.

"No."

"Okay, I'll take care of it."

"Thanks, Tom." Brett hung up.

CHAPTER THIRTY-FOUR

Andrews clicked off from his phone call and slipped his phone back into his pocket. He scratched at the side of his short blond hair and looked at Ben Miglin, who sat at his desk, staring back at us.

"What can you tell us about closed or terminated accounts?" Andrews asked.

"What do you want to know?" Miglin asked.

"Just an overview on how they are handled from the moment they are closed or terminated."

Miglin cleared his throat. "Well, general closed accounts—meaning closed by the user—get compiled into a batch. We send out an automated e-mail to them at the end of the month in which they were closed, with a survey. It asks why they left and invites them to come back."

I had an immediate question but allowed him to continue.

"Terminated accounts are kept on file by the IP address so if the user tries to sign up again, they can get autodenied."

"So there are records of both?" I asked.

He nodded. "Of course."

I was confused because Bailor had said specifically that they didn't keep that information.

"Is there a way to access the list of e-mails and names?" Andrews asked. "Can the accounts be reinstated?"

"Um, yeah, but it requires administrative access. If a user calls and their account was hacked or something, or maybe terminated by mistake, we obviously have to be able to look them up and get them reinstated. Also, if a user who canceled themselves decides to come back and use the site again, we have to be able to put everything back the way it was."

"What about the messages sent and received through the messaging app?" I asked. "Do those come back as well?"

"Yeah, everything gets restored as it was," Miglin said.

"Can you look up a name on an account for us and get it reinstated if it needs to be?" I asked. "We need to see messages from it."

"Ah," he said. "I think I should probably let someone with a bit more, um, authority I guess, make the call on doing that."

"We have a subpoena for the information on the user," Andrews said.

"Okay, um. Still, I'm really not in a position to be doing that kind of stuff. I'd need someone to give me the okay."

"Understandable," Andrews said. "Did you want to call a manager or something?"

"We don't really have managers. Everyone on this

floor reports directly to Mr. Bailor."

The door at our back opened. A man dressed in a dark-gray suit and red tie stood before us in the doorway. His hair was dark and thin, his face weathered.

"Tom Mears. I'm the chief legal officer here at Classified OD. Can I help you gentlemen with something?"

I looked at Andrews. I knew immediately what the guy was there to do—make sure we didn't get another word out of Ben Miglin.

"We're conducting an investigation, and it appears our subpoenas weren't sufficiently taken care of," Andrews said.

"As far as I know, we provided you with that information yesterday. Do you have anything official I could look at that says they weren't sufficiently fulfilled?" he asked.

Andrews didn't respond.

"Do you have some paperwork for me or anything, for that matter, that gives you a legal right to be on the premises, questioning the staff?"

Andrews smirked. "We have a federal subpoena for information and believe that additional information was withheld."

"Okay. Your belief doesn't actually give you a right to question this man sitting here, so I'm going to ask you gentlemen to leave our business. When you have warrants, more subpoenas, or the legal right to question one of our employees, we'd be happy to accommodate you."

Andrews cracked his neck from side to side and walked from the office. I followed. The attorney did his best security-guard routine to make sure we got on the elevator. We rode down in silence. The conversation that we were about to have wasn't for the other elevator riders. We stepped from the elevator and rode the escalators down to the lobby. Andrews and I stepped outside and walked toward our car.

The streets of downtown were cool. I didn't know if that was due to our proximity to Lake Michigan or the streets being in the shadows of the towering high-rises. I chalked it up to a combination of both.

"What a weasel," Andrews said.

"The lawyer?" I asked.

"Yeah, I despise attorneys. That guy was about to give us exactly what we needed."

We stopped and waited for the signal to change to cross the road.

I leaned against the streetlight pole and shrugged. "Which is exactly why the attorney showed up to stop him. And I'm guessing the attorney was sent by Bailor. What did he say on the phone?"

"Reiterated that they didn't keep the information."

"So he bullshitted you some more?"

"Yup. He's on the phone telling me that it's not possible, and two seconds later, the guy sitting in front of us tells me it is."

The walk signal lit, and we crossed the street.

"Bailor is doing one of two things," I said, "either trying to hide the fact that his business was used to murder women—which if that's the case, he's obstructing a murder investigation—or he's the one killing them."

"That's a big presumption. Owner of a giant corporation by day, serial killer by night."

"Not really. Take his job and money out of it. The guy

has access to the system we think the women and our killer were using, he's lying to us, and he's the lead web developer, meaning he's probably capable of creating the virus or knows somebody who could."

"Well, the same could probably be said about anyone who works in the web-development division of the company."

"Except two things. One, Bailor is lying to us. Two, something Kennedy Taylor's sister said."

"What's that?"

"The guy Kennedy was talking to was older and had money. She mentioned a Ferrari. Bailor has money, and to a twenty-something-year-old woman, a forty-something-year-old man would qualify as older. Also, a third thing. He's a suit-and-tie type, which is in line with the man who met with Rebecca for coffee."

We entered the parking structure and walked to the car. Andrews stuck his key in the door to unlock it. "I get you," he said. "What's the move? Do we want to try to bring him in for questioning?"

I shook my head and opened the door. Andrews and I both got in.

"No. No bringing him in. He'll show up with an entourage of attorneys, and we won't get squat. You said he wasn't in the office until Monday, huh?"

"That's what they said, yeah."

"See where he lives. Maybe we can catch him at home. My afternoon is free," I said.

Andrews smiled, clicked a few buttons on his car's computer's keypad, and brought up Brett Bailor's information on the screen. "Looks like he lives out in Lemont."

"Where's that?" I asked.

"About an hour from here."

"Does he have a Ferrari registered to him?"

"One second." Andrews clicked a few buttons on the car's computer. "No. Just a Jeep."

"Do you need to be back for anything?" I asked. "If you do, I can head out there solo or wait for Beth."

"No. I don't have anything other than this. We can head out there now if you want," Andrews said.

"Point us there. I'm going to call Beth and leave her a message letting her know we are going that way."

Andrews started the car and pulled from the parking structure. I dialed Beth, expecting to get her voice mail, but she picked up right away.

"Great minds think alike," she said.

"Huh?" I asked.

"I was just about to call you. I just left Hilary Wormack's house. I have her daughter's computer in my hand."

"Oh. Good. I figured I was going to get your voice mail. I wanted to let you know that we are driving out to Brett Bailor's place."

"For?"

"Everything he's been feeding us about not being able to get information from canceled or terminated accounts is bullshit. One of his employees told us straight out that you could. This is right before we got asked to leave the building by the company's attorney."

"Interesting. Is he now a suspect?"

"Well, I'd like to go and have a chat with him. Andrews and I are just leaving downtown for his home. I guess he didn't feel like showing for work today."

"Where does Bailor live?" Beth asked.

I cupped the mouthpiece of the phone and looked at Andrews. "What town does he live in, again?"

"Lemont," Andrews said.

I brought my cell phone back to my mouth. "Lemont. I think it's about an hour from where we are now."

"Lemont is literally two minutes away from where I'm at. Send me over the address. I'll meet you guys there."

"Okay. Don't approach him until we get there."

"Yeah, I'll wait. No problem," she said.

"We'll see you in a bit." I hung up.

After I got the address from the car's computer and sent it over to Beth, I stuffed my phone back into my pocket. "She's going to meet us there."

Andrews nodded.

We entered the on-ramp for the freeway a few minutes later. The more the details from the investigation played in my mind, the more I thought of Bailor as a likely suspect. Rattling around in my head was a piece of information I'd absorbed somewhere, sometime, about CEOs having psychopathic tendencies and how their lack of empathy helped them in a corporate setting. My cell phone vibrated against my leg, breaking my train of thought. I pulled it out and looked at the screen—Beth was calling.

"Yeah?" I answered.

"I have a Ferrari in the driveway," she said.

"No shit? Black?"

"Yup. I'm looking at it right now."

"Okay. Does it look like he's there?" I asked.

"The garage is open. I didn't see him though."

"All right. We'll be there in what, forty minutes, Andrews?"

He looked at me. "A bit less."

"Less than forty minutes, Beth," I said.

"Okay," she said.

I looked back at Andrews. "There's a black Ferrari in the driveway."

"I'm getting more agents out there," Andrews said. "I don't think they'll beat us there, but if Bailor is the killer, I want more than three of us there to take him down."

"Hear that?" I asked Beth.

"Yeah, Andrews is getting more agents out here," she said.

"Hang tight. Make sure he doesn't leave, but stay the hell away from him. We'll be there in a bit."

"Shit," Beth said.

"What?"

"He's behind my car."

"What? Drive away," I said.

"Shit," Beth repeated.

"Beth, leave now, go."

She didn't respond.

"Agent," a man said, "um, obvious question: why are you parked in front of my home?"

"Damn. Bailor is talking to her." I muted my phone and clicked it onto speaker so Andrews and I could both hear the conversation.

CHAPTER THIRTY-FIVE

Brett walked out to the garage, passed his Jeep, and opened the driver's door of the Ferrari. He ducked his head as he got inside and behind the wheel. He clicked the button on the remote attached to the visor, to lift the garage door. He fired up the motor and tapped the gas, and the roar echoed through the garage. Brett shifted into reverse and began backing up. He looked back over his shoulder and pulled out.

Brett thumbed the button again, to close the garage door.

He patted his pockets.

"Son of a bitch," he said. "Wallet."

Brett hit the button on the garage remote again, sending the door back up. He clicked the car into park and got out. After heading inside, he found his wallet sitting on the nightstand of the master bedroom and scooped it up. Then he headed back through the house and out through the open garage door, and something caught his attention from the corner of his eye. A car had parked just outside the front gates of his property. Brett's was the only house on a dead-end road. He craned his neck and then took a few steps toward the front of the house. Brett's house was on a bit of a hill, sitting higher than the street below. The front gates were a hundred yards down the driveway. The farther Brett walked toward the front door of the house, the better his view became. The car was a newer blue sedan.

Brett started down the driveway toward the street.

The rear of the car came into full view. He stood at the edge of his front gates and looked through the back glass of the car. A single person was inside, a woman. Brett walked around the side of the gate and hopped a short cement wall with a stone facade that surrounded the front of his property along the street. He noticed a sticker from a rental-car company applied to the corner of the trunk lid and walked to the driver's-side. The woman inside was a brunette. She was talking on the phone. Brett banged his knuckles on the window.

The woman's head quickly turned to look at him, and she tossed the phone on the passenger seat of the car.

Brett yanked his head back in shock. The driver was the female FBI agent he'd seen the day prior.

She lowered her window.

"Agent," Brett said, "um, obvious question: why are you parked in front of my home?"

"Oh, hello, Mr. Bailor."

Brett waited for the agent to reply to his question—she didn't.

"Again, I have to ask the nature of your visit," Brett said.

The woman seemed to stumble for words. "I just wanted to follow up with you on a few things."

"Those things being?" he asked.

"Just a few discrepancies regarding what you have told us and what an employee had told the other agents that visited your office—that is, before they were asked to leave by your corporate attorney."

"Asked to leave?" he asked.

The woman nodded.

"Well, that order didn't come from me. I haven't been in today and haven't spoken to anyone on my staff aside from my intern, and that was me chewing him out for not getting a set of transcripts over to one of your other agents."

"Okay," she said. The woman went quiet.

Brett wondered why she seemed to be stalling, sitting inside the car.

"Are you going to get out and ask me these questions or what? Did you want to go up to the house? I'm kind of pressed for time."

"Um, I actually need a few minutes here. I need to make a couple of phone calls," she said.

"Well, I'm going to have to ask you to schedule something with my secretary, then. I have a lunch meeting that I need to be at."

The woman shut off the car and grabbed her phone and a file from the passenger seat. She opened the driver's door and stepped out. "I guess my calls will have to wait, then. This is time sensitive."

Brett shook his head and started for the house, but the woman lingered at the end of the driveway.

Brett stopped and looked back at her. "Are you coming?"

She looked reluctant but started walking his way.

He spoke to her over his shoulder. "How long is this going to take? If I need to reschedule my lunch meeting, I'm going to need a time."

"Um, it shouldn't take too long," she said.

Brett continued up the driveway without responding.

"Nice car," the agent said. "What is that? A Ferrari?"

"Yeah. It's a rental." He opened the front door and stepped inside the house. The woman followed him in, and Brett closed the door at her back.

"Wow, nice place," she said.

"Yeah. Thanks."

"We need a place we can sit and go over this," she said.

"That will work." She started for the living room.

Brett glanced to where she was headed. The wine glass Monica had been drinking from still sat on the edge of the table. He could have passed it off as his own if it weren't for the red lipstick around the rim. Brett figured keeping the agent away from it, and any questions about it, would be best.

"Over here. We'll sit at the kitchen island," Brett said.

The woman stopped, turned, and walked to where Brett was taking a seat.

She sat two stools away from him, opened the folder she had, and flipped through the papers within.

Brett stared at her for a silent minute. She didn't look as though she was looking for anything in particular.

"I'm sorry. I don't remember your name from yesterday," Brett said.

"Agent Harper," she said. She didn't take her eyes from the papers in the folder.

Brett continued watching the woman—she was clearly stalling.

"These questions?" he asked. "I'm pressed for time."

"Right, sorry. I'm just trying to get organized here."

Brett cracked his knuckles.

The woman looked up from her papers and stared across the kitchen near the stove. "Wine connoisseur?" she asked.

Brett glanced over at the bottles in the rack and dismissed her comment.

"That container with the bow-tie pasta in it is cute," she said.

"Let's get on with this," he said. "I don't have all day."

Agent Harper flipped one of the papers in the folder over to give herself a clean page. "Sure. Tell me why one of your employees would say that terminated and canceled accounts are in fact retrievable when you have told us on multiple occasions that they aren't?" She held a pen against the paper, waiting for his answer.

"He's mistaken. You used to be able to, but we made some changes a while back to increase our bottom line a bit. The costs associated with storing all the information were too high to justify continuing in that way." Brett said, lying blatantly.

"Right." The woman wrote something down on the paper. "When were these changes made?"

"Second quarter of this year."

"Second quarter is when?"

"April to June."

"So just before these women became victims."

Brett shrugged. "Yeah, I guess."

The agent cocked her head to one side. She tucked her brown hair behind her right ear. "Strikes me as odd. The time line there is coincidental."

"Yeah, I don't know. What are you insinuating? That a financial move by my company to help the bottom line was done to destroy information from these women?"

"I just said that it was odd. So you're saying that there definitely isn't a way to reinstate closed accounts?"

"That's what I'm telling you."

The woman scooted around a bit on the stool. She flipped the folder closed. "Maybe the living room would be better. These stools are kind of hard." She stood, took the file, and started for the living room.

Brett shook his head as the woman looked from side to side. She was taking in everything in the room. Something was off. He thought of all her actions since he saw her parked in front of his home—her stalling, her questions about the wine and pasta, the car, the fact she was even there. Brett rose from his stool and followed.

The agent stopped in the center of the living room. "Have some female company lately?" She nodded toward the wine glass. "Looks like someone spilled a bit." She reached inside her blazer with her right hand.

He took several lunging steps toward her, his feet thumping. The agent dropped the file she carried, the papers inside falling from within and floating through the air to the floor. She spun toward him, trying to free her weapon from the holster under her arm. Brett delivered a right fist to her face. The agent flew back and fell to the floor, tripping over the edge of the coffee table. Her left arm sent the wine glass and miscellaneous knickknacks on the table's surface flying. The woman tried to pull herself to her feet while removing her gun. Brett grabbed her by her hair and lifted her.

"It's him!" the woman screamed.

He spun her in his arms and wrapped his left arm around her neck. She tried getting out another scream but was cut off when his left arm found its mark under her chin. She flailed for her weapon, finally removing it from her holster. Brett's right hand met her weapon as soon as she pulled it. She fired a single shot into the living room tile, but Brett easily disarmed her. He grabbed his elbow to increase the pressure on the choke hold. The woman kicked her feet and scratched at his arms. Her hands pawed off the sides of his face. Her feet kicked at the coffee table.

Brett shook her back and forth while squeezing her throat between his forearm and bicep. She struggled frantically for another few seconds before going lethargic and then limp. Brett dropped her to the ground and went through her pockets. He felt a phone and removed it. The call timer was running—it showed a duration of twenty minutes to an Agent Rawlings.

He brought the phone to his mouth. "Better hurry," he said and hung up.

Brett scooped up her gun, tucked it into the back of his waistline, and grabbed Agent Harper by the arm. He pulled her across the tile toward the basement door.

CHAPTER THIRTY-SIX

Andrews was heavy on the gas pedal. The car's lights and siren were on full song. Beth being alone in the house with Bailor was troubling. Andrews had just finished contacting the local PD and requesting their assistance at the scene. I hoped they would beat us there.

Andrews and I had been listening to Beth and Bailor's conversation for ten minutes. Her voice sounded different—hesitant or downright scared, I didn't know which. She'd never mentioned that we or other agents were on the way. However, she'd been making obvious comments about things she'd seen inside the home.

"How far away are we?" I asked.

"Ten minutes yet," Andrews said. "She needs to back off a bit. She's questioning things that she shouldn't be questioning."

Andrews's radio came alive. We heard the local PD being dispatched. The sound of the radio blocked some of what Beth was saying to Bailor. It sounded as though she mentioned wine again.

"This guy is going to know something is up if she

continues much more," Andrews said.

As soon as the words left his mouth, we heard static and rustling noises coming from Beth's end of the call, and she screamed, "It's him!"

"Shit!" I said.

What followed next was worse. Andrews and I heard what could only have been a gunshot.

Neither of us spoke.

We heard more muffled sounds coming from Beth's end of the call. I looked down at the screen and clicked the button to unmute the call. "Beth?" I asked.

"Better hurry," a man's voice said in response.

The line went dead.

Andrews stared at me.

"Get everyone there now," I said.

Andrews got on the phone and started dialing as the car's transmission downshifted and the motor revved. After Andrews made the calls, we didn't speak until we slid to a stop in front of a pair of gates and Beth's rental car. I looked around. Aside from Beth's car, there was nothing—no local PD and no other federal cars. We were the only ones there.

"Where the hell is everybody?" I asked.

"On their way." He pulled his service weapon and bailed out of the driver's side of the car. I did the same on the passenger's side.

Andrews and I rushed toward Bailor's property. Halfway up the driveway, the full house came into view, a giant single-story brick home with four individual garage doors facing the driveway. The Ferrari was sitting near an open garage door. Andrews stopped short and pointed toward the front door. We rushed to it, him covering me while I tried the handle—locked. The door was big and looked to be crafted from hardwood. We went for the open garage door.

I covered Andrews as he stayed low, entering the garage.

"Looks empty," he said.

To our immediate right was a white four-door Jeep that looked to be set up for off-road duty. On our left were garage bays filled with lawn-mowing equipment and a four wheeler. We went farther in, past the Jeep. On the right hand side wall was a flight of stairs leading down, and a door that I assumed headed inside stood just next to the stairwell. I checked the door leading in—open.

"Let's go," Andrews said.

I nodded and pushed the door open, and we went in. A large foyer spread out before us. The big, locked front door was twenty feet to my right—to my left, a huge living room with a vaulted ceiling. The back of the room was glass and looked out onto a patio attached to the back of the house—beyond the patio was a woods. My eyes came back to the living room itself, and I noticed papers scattered across the floor. The living room coffee table was off center and the items on top of it strewn about. The papers and state of the coffee table suggested a struggle.

I pointed toward the area.

Andrews nodded.

My head swiveled left and right. The house was silent—I heard nothing and saw no movement from anywhere. We went farther in, weapons drawn and ready. I took quick, crouched steps to the kitchen, cleared it, and went back through to Andrews covering me in the living room. We moved from the living room to search the rooms coming off of the hall.

The hallway contained five doors, all open. I quickly cleared the first two, a bathroom and a home office. The following two rooms on the left and right were also empty—both spare bedrooms, one of which looked to be themed for a young boy. We continued to the final door and entered. A large master-bedroom suite spread out to our left and right. The windows on the left of the room faced the driveway, and to our right was a patio area with walk-out doors. We walked through and checked the large closet and master bath—both empty.

"That flight of stairs in the garage probably led down to the basement," Andrews said.

We worked our way back through the house, still seeing no one.

"One of these doors has to lead down," I said.

The second door we tried near the kitchen led down a flight of stairs. The lights were on below. Andrews and I took the stairs down, quietly. We rounded the corner to the right—a large game room took up the area, with a pair of pool tables in the center and dartboards against the wall. A bar was to my right and a theater area next to it. The room was empty. We continued through, to a door at the back. Andrews reached for the knob and pushed the door open. We entered a short hallway. To our right was a home gym loaded with fitness equipment but empty of people. A cedar door to our left led to a sauna. We continued to the door at the end of the hall. Andrews opened it to a large dark room. He reached inside along the wall for a light switch. As soon as the lights came on, my eyes immediately shot to the left. In the wide-open storage area, a woman lay in her undergarments upon a silver table near a washbasin—Beth. The cement wall behind her was covered with pieces of paper. Andrews stepped into the room and swung his weapon left and right. The room was empty aside from miscellaneous items in totes, a washer and dryer, and Beth. I holstered my weapon. Andrews and I ran to her.

"Shit," I said.

Her body looked pale. I noticed bruising around her neck and swelling on the right side of her face. Beth lay with tubes coming from her neck, legs, and arms. Blood was flowing freely from her, through the tubes, to a drain in the floor. I jammed two fingers next to a tube on the right side of her throat. Her skin was cold and clammy. Through my fingertips, I felt a weak pulse.

"She's still alive. Get paramedics here, now," I said. "I'm getting these tubes out of her."

Andrews pulled his phone from his pocket.

I grabbed the two needles and tubes attached at her legs and slid them out, then I went to her arms and then to the tubes along the sides of her neck. The gauge of the needles was large. Blood continued to pour from the entry points of the needles after they were removed.

"I'm not getting any signal," Andrews said. "I need to get outside and call."

"Go."

Andrews jogged to the door on our right. He opened it, walked through, and disappeared. It must have been the one that led up into the garage.

I stuck my fingers over the holes in the sides of her neck, trying to limit the blood loss. My eyes went to the right, where blood was pooling near her legs.

"Shit," I said. "Hang on, Beth." I took a hand from the side of her neck and tried shaking her head by the chin. She didn't respond, and as soon as my hand left the side of her neck, the blood began to flow again. I needed to get something on the wounds. My eyes darted back and forth around the room, and I caught a clear view of the papers and photographs covering the wall. A few of the girls' faces in the photos looked familiar. My eyes left the wall and continued searching. I spotted a roll of tape on a shelf, and I went to it and tried to peel off a strip. With my bloody hands, I couldn't get the tape to come free of the roll. I frantically wiped the blood from my hands on my suit and scratched my fingernail against the edge of the tape roll until a piece came up. I ripped it off with my teeth and tried sticking it to her neck—it wouldn't stay.

"Shit," I said again. I needed to get the wounds covered or find something to tie around the wounds to limit the blood flow. I set the roll of tape on Beth's midsection and loosened my tie. I ripped it from my shirt collar and tied it around one of Beth's legs—something I had done before. "Andrews!" I called.

No response.

I needed another tie—or anything. I looked around, trying to find Beth's clothes or something to use. I spotted nothing other than the tubes I'd just removed from her.

"Tubes," I said.

I scooped them up from the ground and began tying them around her other leg and arms. Blood sprayed from the tubes' ends as I tightened them down. All I needed was something for her neck—fast.

I grabbed the left sleeve of my suit jacket with my right hand. With four hard yanks, it ripped free. I lifted Beth's head and slipped the sleeve under and around her neck. I circled her neck with the tape roll five or six times until the fabric was tight but not choking her.

"Andrews!" I called again. "What's up with those paramedics?"

I again received no response.

I took Beth in my arms and carried her from the house the way Andrews had just left. I walked her up the flight of stairs into the garage and carried her around the front of the Jeep, where I stopped dead in my tracks. Andrews lay just outside the garage door on the ground. Blood covered the back of his head and colored the white collar of his shirt red.

I immediately knelt and lay Beth on the ground. Then I pulled my service weapon, stayed crouched, and went to Andrews. I looked around but spotted no one. As soon as my fingers touched his throat to check for a pulse, he came to. He immediately tried to break free from me and patted his hands over his body.

"It's Rawlings," I said. "What happened? Where is he?"

"I don't know. I came out of the garage and got hit with something." He touched the top back area of his head and then looked at the blood on his hand.

"Stay put. Watch Beth. Did you get off the call to paramedics?"

"No. I don't know where my phone is." He searched left to right.

"Do you have your gun?" I asked.

Andrews patted his holster and then looked around. "Under the Jeep," he said. "It must have flown from my hand."

I pulled out my cell phone, dialed 9-1-1, and handed the phone to Andrews. "Get them here," I said.

I stood and looked down the driveway. Both of Bailor's vehicles were still there. The driveway gate was closed, and our car blocked the outside of the gates. Through the trees, I saw a car coming up the street and figured that to be some of our backup arriving—either local PD or more agents.

"People are coming. I'm going after Bailor," I said. "You didn't see which way he went?"

"No," he said.

I looked around. My options were any direction other than through the front. I jogged to the side of the garage to look toward the back of the house. The grass that wrapped the home turned into woods just fifty feet from the home's edges. I spotted a trail leading back into the woods. I followed the trail with my eyesight, and something caught my eyes through the tops of the trees and down the hill a bit—a clearing and what looked like an aluminum roof. I ran to the trail, which immediately turned left as soon as it entered the woods. Straight ahead, down the hill, I had a clear visual on the building—a red pole shed with multiple garage doors facing the trail, which was grass and mud under my feet but turned into a gravel service road of some sort at the front of the building and continued on in the other direction. One of the garage doors on the front of the outbuilding lifted before my eyes. I picked up a full run—the building stood just a hundred yards away. My feet thumped the muddy ground, sliding a bit with each footstep.

"FBI! Brett Bailor! Come out with your hands in the air!"

The man looked out from the open garage door—it was definitely Bailor. A gun came up. I dove to the tree line and tried to get low. Bailor fired six shots in succession, all entering the woods around me. Branches snapped, and bark and leaves fell on my shoulders. I jammed a knee down into the mud and brought myself up to a firing position. Bailor spun back into the garage, gone from my gun's sights. I stood, hugged the tree line along the left side of the trail, and continued advancing, the garage door just thirty yards away. I could see inside the building at an angle. The lights were off, but several vehicles appeared to be stored under covers within.

I heard the sound of an engine firing up, followed by a screech of tires. A black sedan shot from the front of the pole shed, and the rear end of the car slid to the right, throwing gravel into the air. I brought my weapon up and emptied the magazine through the car's passenger side and back glass. The nose of the car dove to the left and found a three-foot-wide oak tree, dead center. The car's rear tires rose from the ground upon collision. I heard an explosion from the airbags as the vehicle made impact. I dropped the magazine from my weapon, inserted another, and chambered a round as I ran over. I heard a single gunshot and saw what looked like a muzzle flash from inside the car. Pink colored the white smoke that hung inside the vehicle.

"Shit!" Approaching low and from the side of the car, I could see the man inside.

"Bailor! Out of the car! Hands where I can see them!" I figured it to be a useless command but said it regardless.

I stood outside the passenger door, my gun pointed in. Bailor lay hunched over, against the driver's door. The car's airbag, wet with blood, lay half over his face. His eyes were open staring down, unblinking. Blood covered the vehicle's headliner. I kept my gun pointed in and opened the passenger door. Still, he didn't move.

"Bailor!" I shouted.

Nothing.

I could see his right hand but not his left. He wasn't holding a weapon with his right though I saw a gun in the passenger-side footwell. I removed the weapon from the car and took a few steps back. Keeping aim on him as I walked around the front of the car and the tree, which was lodged into it, I stopped upon reaching the driver's side of the vehicle and holstered my weapon. I could clearly see an exit wound on the top left of Bailor's head. A sound caught my ear as I stared at Bailor. Local police were jogging down the trail toward me, weapons drawn.

"I'm Agent Rawlings, FBI," I said. I held up empty hands toward them.

"You need paramedics down here?" one of the officers shouted.

"No," I said. "We need them up top for the female agent."

I walked toward the trio of officers standing on the passenger side of the car.

"They're with her now," one of the officers said.

CHAPTER THIRTY-SEVEN

I left the black sedan, Bailor's body, and the local PD at the pole shed and made my way back up to the house. An ambulance had backed up just outside the garage, its rear doors open, and two patrol cars had pulled into the driveway. I glanced down toward the street. The front gates were open, the car Andrews and I had driven, had been pulled to the far side of the road. I looked into the garage. The Paramedics had Beth on a gurney inside. Two men stood at her sides. I also spotted Andrews leaning against the hood of the Jeep, holding a bloody rag against the top of his head.

I walked inside. "Is she going to be okay?"

The man on the right turned back toward me, and as he moved, I saw Beth staring at me.

"I'll be fine," she said.

"You're awake? And talking?" I asked.

"Looks like it."

"We need to get fluids in her to replenish the blood loss," one of the EMTs said. "I take it the sleeve over the wounds on her neck came from you?"

I looked down at my one-sleeved, suit jacket and nodded.

"It helped, without a doubt," he said.

"Yeah, another few minutes, and we would have been dealing with something else here entirely," the other EMT said. "If those were what were in her." He nodded at the tubes I'd used to tie off her arms and legs, lying on the floor of the garage.

I stood at her side. Beth lifted her head a bit, to get a better look at me. "Is that all my blood?"

"Yeah," I said.

"Sorry."

"I'll let it slide this time. Next time, you're getting me a new suit."

Beth smiled, but looked weak. Her voice was low and strained. "My eye hurts worse than anything, my throat being second."

"Do you remember what happened?" I asked.

"Yeah. When he came to the car, I just let my phone run, hoping you would be listening in on the conversation."

"Yeah, Andrews and I heard the whole thing."

"Well, I was trying to stall him but just kept saying the worst things. I told you I'm not a good talker under pressure, especially since I knew it was him the second I got into the house. When I walked out to the living room, I saw a wine glass and spilled wine on the carpet. I mention it, and he doesn't respond. Well, as I'm reaching into my blazer pocket for a piece of gum, I hear footsteps pounding behind me. I drop everything, turn toward him, and go for my weapon. He put a fist in my face, sending me over the coffee table before I could get it out. I went for my gun again, but he got to me first and got an arm around my neck. I got my weapon out, but it was too late. He had me in a choke hold. I screamed it was him, hoping you were still listening on the other end of the phone. I woke up on this gurney."

"Okay," I said. "You don't remember being in his basement?"

"No."

A few feet away, Andrews cleared his throat. "Good. Don't."

"I heard one of the officer's radio say he was dead," Beth said.

I nodded and gave her the short version. "I had him down in the pole shed. He took off in a car. I fired on it. He crashed and then shot himself." I put my hand, fashioned like a gun, under my chin and brought my thumb down.

She nodded.

I looked at the EMT. "When are you heading out with her?"

"Now."

"And to what hospital?"

"Silver Cross in New Lenox," he said.

"Address?" I asked. I patted the inside pocket of my one-sleeved, blood-covered suit jacket for my notepad.

"I know where it is," Andrews said. "I might have to go there and get stitched up, I think. Damn head won't stop bleeding." He inspected the rag he was holding against his head. "You can give me a ride as soon as we take care of everything here."

I looked back at one of the EMTs. "How long is she going to be there?"

"Probably just overnight. We'll take some X-rays and keep running fluids."

"I'll meet you over there in a bit, Beth."

"Okay," she said. "Just make sure we get everything from here. Call Ball and let him know."

"I will."

The EMTs wheeled Beth from the garage to the awaiting ambulance. I went to Andrews at the front of the Jeep. "Do we have anyone else here yet?"

"No. I'd imagine any minute."

"All right. I need to go and check out that wall downstairs quick. We're going to need a forensics team in here. If you need to go and get stitched up, you should probably do it."

"I'll be fine, and forensics is on the way. You're talking about the wall with the papers and photos?"

"Yeah, some looked familiar," I said.

Andrews and I headed down the steps from the garage to the basement. We walked to where Beth had been lying. Both of us stared at the cinder-block wall behind the stainless-steel table. I counted over twenty photographs. Each one was of a woman in a state of undress and apparently dead. Many of them had the same—or a similar—stainless-steel table beneath their bodies. Tubes came from the women in about half of the photos. Taped to the wall behind each photo was a piece of paper. I got closer and read a number of them. The latest ones were all the same—a copy of a man's personals listing. I recognized the most recent victims photos attached to each. Some of the older ones looked like copies from people either buying or selling something.

"It's a damn trophy wall," I said.

Andrews let out a breath. He took the bloody rag from his head, inspected it, and then jammed it into his pocket. "Disgusting, but a whole pile of evidence."

I moved to the left to inspect some of the older photos and listings. My eyes caught a date at the bottom corner of a photo. I looked left to right—some of the photos were dated, and some weren't. I found the oldest date I could. "Nineteen ninety-four."

Andrews turned toward me, taking his attention from the items sitting upon the shelves next to the washbasin. "I don't think the classified website started until the early two thousands."

"Yeah, these older ads look like something you would post on a cork board. We have some that look like they were clipped and copied from a newspaper."

"So he's been at this a while. Just changing to keep with the times."

"Guess so," I said.

"Are there names on any of the sheets behind the photos?"

"No. It doesn't look like it. We're going to have to try to find out who these older ones are. Anything over there?"

"A couple of cell phones. Miscellaneous garbage on the top and bottom shelf. Bleach, gloves, a Polaroid camera with a photo sticking out of it on this one." He lifted his chin to get a better look of the picture. "The photo is of Beth. We might have interrupted him when we came in."

"Just a damn good thing we got here when we did. Did the forensic team give you an ETA?"

"They should be here any minute."

"Okay." I stepped back from inspecting the wall. "Let's leave all of this for them and step outside."

We headed back out through the garage. Agent Toms was standing with a group of patrol officers in the driveway. Andrews and I walked over.

"Is Agent Harper going to be okay?" Toms asked.

"It looks like it," I said.

"So the gazillionaire owner of Classified OD is our serial killer?"

"Without a doubt," I said.

"How does that happen? I mean, you can have anything with the amount of money this guy had."

"It looks like he was doing this prior to starting the business. There's photos in the basement dating back to ninety-four," Andrews said.

Agent Toms didn't respond.

"Forensics?" Andrews asked.

"Nick is down at the street with one of his guys. Should be up any second, I'd think," Agent Toms said.

"Andrews, when they get up here, do you want to show them around a bit?" I asked. "I need to make a call back to my home office quick."

"Sure. You'll probably need this." Andrews reached into his pocket, pulled out my cell phone, and passed it over.

"I'm sure it would help." I gave Andrews a nod and dialed Ball back in Manassas. He picked up within a few rings.

"Ball," he said.

"Hey, it's Rawlings."

"I was wondering when I was going to get an update from you."

"Ah. We found him. He's dead," I said.

"Certain?" he asked.

I scratched at the back of my hair, freeing a couple of wood splinters that I assumed had come from a bullet shattering a tree. "Certain on both accounts. It was definitely him, and he's definitely dead."

"Tell me what happened," Ball said.

I let out a long breath and went into the day for him, start to finish. The call lasted the better part of a half hour. I paced the driveway as I spoke and watched Andrews lead the forensics guys into the house. He came back out and waited ten minutes for me to finish my call. The bloody rag he had been holding against his head earlier made a reappearance. When I finished, I clicked off from Ball and gave my attention to Andrews.

"Forensics guys have it under control. Everything from the place will be gathered and taken back to the field office," Andrews said. "I'm going to leave the scene with Agent Toms. Think I could bother you for that ride to the hospital?"

CHAPTER THIRTY-EIGHT

Wednesday afternoon, I sat in front of my desk computer. Beth and I had flown back the previous Sunday, as planned. Ball told her to take a few days off at the beginning of the week, which she refused. My week had been mostly spent going through everything we'd received from Bailor's houses. The trophy wall we'd found in Lemont, full of photos and classified listings, wasn't his only one. We had matching trophy walls in the basements of his home outside St. Louis and another in a Columbus, Ohio suburb. We had photos of fifty-four deceased women—only fifteen had been killed via the tubes and blood draining. Others were strangulation, knife wounds, and blunt-force trauma.

He'd given us most of the information we needed to place identities on the victims. All the listings that it seemed he had responded to were identified—each had an address, e-mail, or phone number to contact. The ones giving us a bit of trouble were the ones where people had responded to his listings though we were beginning to see a little light at the end of the tunnel by working with missing-persons departments and running license plates. The vehicles in Bailor's shed all belonged to prior victims—seven cars total. The car he'd crashed into the tree belonged to the late Kennedy Taylor. Altogether, Beth and I had positively identified over forty victims going back to the early two thousands. However, who knew how many lives Bailor had actually taken.

Andrews had been making a point to dig into Bailor himself. He'd interviewed Bailor's ex-wife Monday and sent me a copy of the lengthy statement she'd given. While she'd had no idea he was actually capable of the acts he'd committed, she included the reason behind the divorce: she believed he'd been drugging her regularly. Her statement read that she would often wake up in the morning, feeling weak with no recollection of the previous night. Aside from waking up in a fog, she'd have what looked like track marks on her arms and legs. As soon as she distanced herself from Bailor, both of the frequent occurrences discontinued. As to why she didn't go to the authorities, she claimed that she couldn't prove anything and needed his money to provide the best life possible for their child. That was a reason, I guess, but not one I was fond of.

I heard the wheels of Beth's chair squeak at my back.

"I think I may be on to another," she said.

I spun my desk chair around to look at her. "Yeah?"

"I just got an e-mail back from a missing-persons unit in Ohio. I think we might have a match here on a woman named Claudia Hamlin. He sent over a couple photos." Beth waved me to her desk.

I walked over to look at the photos.

"This is the photo from Bailor's." Beth brought it up

on her screen and minimized the window so we could see it next to the other one. "See the little mole on her cheek there?" she asked. Beth pointed at the screen and then turned her head and looked at me.

The bruising around Beth's eye was black but fading to a shade of green. "Yeah. I see it," I said. I looked back and forth between Bailor's photo and the other. "That does look like a match. What did they say as far as when she went missing?"

"Late nineties. They basically have nothing, though. The missing-persons report was filed by a mother who lived out of state."

"What was Bailor's listing that accompanied the photo?"

"Um, hold on." Beth turned back to the computer screen. "Looks like a newspaper ad for workout equipment. A treadmill."

"Okay. I'd say try to get a hold of anyone the missing girl had contact with—friends, family, whatever—and try to see if they remember her mentioning anything about shopping for such a thing. Click back to the photo from Bailor."

Beth brought it up.

"Damn, no date on that one."

Beth turned back toward me. "Yeah, this is an older one, I think. It looks like most of the newer ones were the Polaroids. Speaking of which, why the hell would he be using a Polaroid camera?"

I shrugged. "Why the hell would he be murdering people for twenty-some years."

"Good point."

My eyes dropped to her neck—the bruising was

virtually gone. "Looks like you're healing up." I pointed to my neck and then my eye. "Bruising is looking better."

She nodded. "Makeup helps, but it can't go away soon enough. You wouldn't believe the stares I've been getting, walking around with a black eye."

"Yeah, I would. I'd have to say that was probably my most uncomfortable airport visit and plane ride in my life. The looks I was getting from people were not good. The stewardess asking you if you needed to talk to someone was the icing on the cake."

Beth smiled. "I told her the truth."

"Yeah, I don't think she was buying your story. I half expected to be greeted by police when I stepped off of the plane."

"Oh come on, it wasn't that bad."

My cell phone buzzed in my pocket. I slid it out and looked at the screen. "Let me know what you get on the friends-and-family front about that treadmill. This is Karen—third time she's called. Seems like her new position offers a lot of desk time for her to check in on me."

Beth smiled and nodded. She went back to her computer screen. I clicked Talk and headed from the SCUH office to grab a coffee.

"Hey," I said.

"Hey, you. I called a couple times," Karen said. "Are you busy?"

"I'm just getting things taken care of and going through the case we worked. Still trying to get identities for all these victims."

"How's it coming?" she asked.

"Ah, so far, so good. We're almost there."

"Did you get any comments about your tie?"

I turned left at the hall and headed for the lunch room. "Nope. To tell you the truth, I'm not sure I'm entirely on board with the pink tie and pocket square."

"It's stylish, Hank. You want people to notice you there, don't you? It helps with advancement."

I laughed. "Well, seeing as I've been here for a week, I'm not sure I'm in line for moving up that ladder quite yet. Besides that, I'm not sure I want to be noticed for being the guy who wears the pink ties."

Karen laughed. "It's more mauve than pink. Okay, okay, I'll let you dress yourself for a few days, and we'll see how it goes."

"You're the boss," I said. I turned into the lunch room, which was empty.

"Speaking of which, I'm drinking from my mug now."

I smiled. "I figured you'd like that coffee cup."

"Oh, I do. Anyway, just wanted to remind you about dinner later. Try to not be too late."

"I shouldn't be. I'm guessing I'll be home around six."

"Perfect. Maybe dancing after?"

I winced and quickly made up an excuse. "My ankle has been kind of bugging me."

"Weird. First I've heard of it."

"Yup. Must have twisted it sometime today."

"Mmm hmm. See you in a few hours," Karen said. "Love you."

"Love you too, baby." I clicked off, grabbed my coffee, and headed back toward the office. As soon as I found my desk, Agent Ball walked up, holding a ten-inch-tall stack of files.

"Rawlings," he said. "How are we coming on Bailor?"

"It looks like there's a bit left to do with getting identifications on victims, but I'd say pretty well. Beth has what looks like a pretty good lead on another."

"Oh yeah?"

Beth nodded and gave him the quick version of what she'd found.

Ball turned back to me. "Good work out there again, Hank."

"Appreciate that," I said.

"Okay. So when you think you have about as much as you're going to get on Bailor, maybe next week sometime"—Ball set the stack of files down on the edge of my desk—"these will be yours." He tapped the top folder in the stack. "These are all cold investigations but new serial killers in the last couple years. See what you can find. Just plug the investigation number into the computer like I showed you, and it will bring up everything we have in the system."

"Sure, no problem," I said. "Anything else?"

"Yeah. Nice tie," Ball said. "I've been meaning to mention that all day."

Beth spun in her chair and faced us. "Yeah, that is a lovely shade of pink."

"You're screwing with me, right?" I asked.

"No. Looks great." Ball curled a finger beneath his lip as if he was in thought. Then he removed his hand and ran it through his gray hair. "You know, that's damn close to the same color as a car I seen in the parking lot—little pink hybrid number with some Florida plates."

I smiled. "Okay. Ha ha. I'll give you that one because, honestly, it was a pretty good jab on the fly, and I can appreciate that."

"Thanks," Ball said. "Just a guess, but did your wife have a hand in the pink tie selection, Agent Rawlings?"

I smiled. "Yeah, she's in charge of my outfits, but it sounded like she was going to start letting me dress myself."

Ball snorted a laugh and walked from my desk.

I glanced over at Beth who was staring at me.

"You're actually serious, aren't you?" she asked.

I smiled and swiveled my chair back toward my computer.

The End